MW00790348

TYING THE KNOT

TYING THE KNOT

ERIN SCOGGINS

HELIUM PRESS

TYING THE KNOT

A Wedding Crashers Mystery, Book Two

Copyright © 2021 by Erin Scoggins

Published in the United States by Helium Press

ISBN: 978-1-953826-02-2 (paperback)

ISBN: 978-1-953826-03-9 (ebook)

Library of Congress Control Number: 2020923083

Printed in the United States of America

Cover design by Mariah Sinclair

Editing by Stacy Juba

Proofreading by Beth Hale and Virginia Carey

PO Box 97481

Raleigh, North Carolina 27624

www.erinscoggins.com

For Miller, Gibson, and Serena.
Dream big.

1

According to Flat Falls legend, the ladies in my family have always had a flair for being overly dramatic. If the genealogy websites gave out awards for top-notch drama queens, the Wells women would have rocked their sparkling crowns all the way down the genetic line.

When I was a child, my aunt Beverlee would draw me into her lap to recount stories about my great-grandmother, a bootlegger who spent her best days running from the law. She eventually served time for sideswiping a backwoods sheriff with a souped-up Ford filled with her prized moonshine. When she got out of prison, she married him.

"Every woman needs a spectacular story to tell about her life, Glory," Beverlee would say, and we'd spend hours in the shade under a knotty live oak tree in her back yard dreaming of the ruckus I was going to make in the world.

It turns out I didn't make much of a ruckus.

But even though I didn't wind up as a famous news correspondent or an international spy, I did develop a fondness for other people's drama, mostly in the form of an obsession with trashy TV. From the name-calling to the hair-yanking, if a show provided an evening of theatrical commotion, I was there for the whole dazzling spectacle.

"I can't believe you've never watched *Romance Revival*," I said to my neighbor Josie as I motioned toward the television with a brownie-smudged finger. "They plucked a cast of losers from those smutty grocery store tabloids and asked them to duke it out for half a million dollars and the chance to find true love."

"There's no such thing as true love." Josie sniffed.

"Exactly!" I thrust my fist in the air triumphantly. "It's tacky and ridiculous, and you're going to love it."

"I've never played dress-up to watch TV before," Josie replied, tugging at a gauzy feathered hat Beverlee had found buried under a pile of leftover felt in her craft closet. "It's kind of exciting."

Beverlee and I had always treated reality television like other people treat the Academy Awards—with respect, fanfare, and a colossal buffet. Sometimes we even dressed up for the occasion, like when we teased our bangs and scavenged vintage evening gowns for the finale of a show about geeky millionaires who returned to their high schools for prom re-dos. We cheered and cried like we were the ones strolling into smelly gyms in Vera Wang gowns with diamond bracelets dripping from our wrists.

"You're beautiful, dah-ling," I said, reaching out to tap her plastic glass with mine before tossing a sparkly white scarf over my shoulder. I had picked it out from the clearance bin specifically for the show, its iridescent sequins both gaudy and mesmerizing. And like sports fans with their favorite jerseys, I had been wearing it for every episode since the series began.

Romance Revival provided matchmaking for screw-ups, and since Josie and I both identified with that designation, we were dressed to celebrate and armed with a table of snacks that rivaled a Super Bowl party. We both stood ready to binge on carbs and other people's mistakes under the guise of planning a wedding for the winning contestants.

But unlike the other bawdy shows that captured our evenings, I was being paid to view *Romance Revival*.

It was like winning the lottery. I got to eat and watch television. For money.

Josie gestured toward the array of snacks that covered the coffee table. "We have the two most important food groups–salty and sweet."

Earlier that evening, I had crossed the rickety aluminum porch that stretched between our two apartments above the pawnshop, my arms piled high with bags of chips, microwave pizza, and Hostess cupcakes from the gas station. I made myself a nest on the floor in front of Josie's big-screen television with my fancy wedding planning notebook and two plates to contain my game-day munchies.

"Just wait until Beverlee gets here," I replied. "She was experimenting with double stacking trays in her Volkswagen so she didn't have to make more than one trip. I'm not sure your place will be big enough for all of her baking, but you have better furniture and a TV that doesn't lose its cable connection every time you flush the toilet."

Our apartments were the same layout, only reversed, but where mine looked like a poster for rental furnishings, Josie's was overflowing with hand-stitched tapestries and colorful sculptures. Crystals danced from long strands of transparent fishing line next to the open window, and a half-finished abstract painting rested on an easel in the corner, tubes of acrylic paint discarded at its feet. A wisp of incense trailed into the air from the kitchen counter.

But despite Josie's hippie tendencies, she had an affection for modern technology. As a former computer security expert, she liked her electronic toys flashy and expensive.

That included her high-dollar laptop and the giant television mounted to the wall across from the worn denim sofa.

Her screen was easily twice the size of mine, which made Josie's apartment the obvious choice for our viewing party. It also helped that her place was farther away from the dumpster that occupied the alley between the pawnshop and the inlet, so the breeze carried the scent of fresh sea air instead of yesterday's bait.

I sat cross-legged on the floor in front of her television, one hand gripping a mini cheesecake and the other gesturing toward the screen. I checked out the parade of women with gravity-defying cleavage and abnormally long legs sashaying across the stage. "I'm thinking something sinful for the one who could pass for the evil stepsister from a Disney movie."

Josie twisted her strawberry blonde curls into a topknot she secured with a paintbrush before grabbing a tortilla chip. "How are you supposed to pick out a wedding cake for someone you've never met?"

I flipped through the stack of bios I had printed from the show's website. "Hazel Archer is an underwear model who got arrested for riding a donkey naked through the middle of the Thanksgiving Day Parade in New York City. She was protesting because her local coffee shop took goat milk off their menu. What more do I need to know?"

She snorted. "Good point. What about a fudge cake? I've always thought chocolate paired well with scandal."

"Dark chocolate chipotle it is, then," I replied, scribbling in the margin of my notebook. "Spicy, yet sexy."

On screen, Hazel leaned down and plucked a tissue from a box on the glass coffee table, trailing it slowly down her chest. She unleashed a deep, stuttering breath. "It's so hard." She aimed a duck-lipped pout toward the camera. "I'm the victim here. I was just standing up for what I believe in."

"Oh, please," Josie said with an undisguised look of

disgust. "She's trying to live down flashing her boobs by throwing herself, stilettos-first, into a mud pit filled with other people's drama."

"That's the beauty of the show," I replied. "It's a cesspool of lousy decisions, custom-produced to make the rest of us feel better about our pitiful lives."

Reality television had been a constant source of entertainment for me when my husband had turned out to be a loser trapped in a thief's well-muscled body. Some days, watching other people's lives disintegrate was the only thing that got me through.

"Speak for yourself. I only feel better about my life after I eat nachos," she said with a nod toward my notebook. "When is your meeting with the producer?"

I had received a phone call from Mimi Wakefield, the show's producer, two weeks earlier. She asked if my wedding planning business could put together a last-minute set for them to use when they filmed the season's final episodes.

"It will be simple," she said. "I'm sure you can do it in your sleep."

And although I didn't understand why they'd move filming all the way to North Carolina, I wasn't about to refuse a new customer, especially one with deep pockets and Hollywood connections. Before her call, I was contemplating heading down to the retirement center to convince a few geriatric lovebirds they needed to tie the knot before the grim reaper came knocking.

"Sunday," I said, and panic jolted through me at having less than two days to plan a pseudo-wedding for an unidentified bride.

As far as job opportunities went, they didn't get much bigger than this. The publicity alone would make Carolina Weddings a household name in Flat Falls and would give my new company the injection of cash it needed to flourish.

I just had to dodge the jitters and general lack of knowledge and arrange something fabulous.

As an event planner in Raleigh, I had worked with tighter timelines than this, but I had never done it on film.

"What about Blondie?" Josie angled her chin toward an attractive woman seated on the edge of the sofa, tugging at the hem of her almost see-through white linen dress. "What's her story?"

I glanced at my notes and summoned my best television announcer voice. "Our next contestant is Lily Page, wild-child heir of the Page's Pickles fortune."

I had been studying these people for the better part of two weeks, diving into their personal crises like I was preparing for an international trade summit.

The season was halfway over, and they had already eliminated ten contestants during a series of physical and emotional challenges. One woman was sent packing when she refused to let the producer put a live spider in her wedding dress. They tried to convince her it was good luck in some cultures, but she passed out before they could release the tarantula from its glass jar.

Another man bit the dust when he flipped a dune buggy during a combined scavenger hunt and paintball war in the Mojave Desert.

The few contenders that remained were vying for a dream wedding and a cash jackpot that would be awarded on camera in the middle of a romantic set designed by me.

So far, Lily Page was the frontrunner bride-to-be. With long blond hair, rosy cheeks, and perky dimples, she looked like she should be talking up her policy on global warming to a crowd of pageant judges. Instead, she was trying to live down getting caught on camera in a steamy lip-lock with the son of her father's biggest rival in the middle of the pickle packaging plant.

The clip got five million hits in less than two days, which resulted in a drop in Page's Pickles stock prices by more than half. Nothing halts pickle sales faster than a dirty video in a food prep area.

My gaze swung toward a tray overflowing with gherkins and Spanish olives, and I wrinkled my nose. "For her, something tart. What about lemon?"

Josie shook her head. "Too predictable."

I tapped the pencil against my chin. "I've got it. Vanilla cake with buttered popcorn frosting to honor all those people sitting at home on their sofas watching her send her father's company down in flames like it was a day at the theater."

She gave me a high five. "What about the men? Are they a bunch of lawless losers, too?"

I thumbed through my notes. "Well, we've got a former professional surfer who was selling drugs out of his Winnebago and a white-collar criminal who appears to be on very familiar terms with an abacus."

"Maybe I should go on a reality show," Josie said with a wistful sigh. "I can't do much worse than I already have. At least they're putting their emotional baggage out there from the beginning."

"It's a show about finding romance with people who have proved they are idiots or convicts, Josie." I motioned toward the TV. "Not the best place to find a new husband."

She hiked up her pastel floral sundress to expose the black plastic band of the GPS monitor strapped to her ankle. "Do I need to remind you there's nobody on Earth who knows better than I do what a mistake it is to marry a criminal?"

I ducked my head in a quick apology. Even if Josie wanted to fall in love with another felon, she couldn't. She was stuck in this apartment for the foreseeable future while she paid for the sins of marrying the wrong guy to begin with.

'Til death do us part quickly turned into "Until death or when you get me arrested for computer fraud and embezzlement." Apparently, the Feds don't like it when your financial advisor husband cons you into using your login to divert a hundred thousand dollars into his own account.

"That's why we're friends." I beamed. "We have terrible taste in husbands."

Josie acknowledged my contrition by stealing a potato chip from my plate.

"The producer said they're bringing the last few couples to Flat Falls for the final showdown-slash-wedding." I glanced at my notes. "I need to give them what they want."

"Xanax and a daytime Emmy?" she suggested.

I crumbled my napkin and chucked it backward over my shoulder, watching with satisfaction as it bounced off her cheek. "An outstanding wedding planner," I said, focusing my attention back on the screen, where the announcer was ushering out the potential grooms.

When Josie didn't comment, I twisted around to look at her. She sat unmoving on the sofa, her eyes wide and her fair skin even paler than normal.

"Are you okay?" I asked. "Did you eat a bad pickle?"

She didn't respond.

My chest tightened. "What is it, Josie?"

She slid forward until her knees hit the carpet next to me and raised a finger toward the screen. "He's out."

I pointed a cheese puff at the TV. "Who? You recognize that guy?"

Her shoulders sagged as she dropped the rest of the way to the floor. "He's not just a guy, Glory. He was my guy."

"The surfer?" I asked. Out of the four men occupying the red leather sofa in the middle of the stage, he was the only one who seemed in Josie's league. The others were a mish-mash of hair plugs and dad jeans.

She shook her head. "Not that one. The one on the right."

I released a short laugh. "The guy with the bald spot and the sweater vest? Huh. I would have taken you more for a biceps lover, not a 'let's get frisky with your necktie, Mr. President.' He strikes me as an investment—"

Josie threw her foot out, the ankle monitor making a loud clunk against the leg of the coffee table. "Banker," she said. "And he is incredibly charming when you get to know him."

Realization hit me with a sharp punch. "Oh." I gestured toward the man who was smiling at the camera. "That's your husband?"

"Yes," she whispered. "Or at least he was until he threw me under the jail on his way to a lighter sentence."

I leaned back against the edge of the sofa and was about to pepper her with questions when Josie's apartment door flung open.

Beverlee Wells-Bartholomew, my aunt and the woman who raised me after both my parents died, pushed into the room carrying a gingham-lined picnic basket brimming with foil packages. Dressed in a yellow floral romper with matching platform sandals, she resembled an over-ripe lemon. "Good, I haven't missed anything."

Josie rolled her eyes. "Come on in, Beverlee."

"Scoots is running to the shop for more snacks." Beverlee kicked off her sandals and wiggled her toes in Josie's tan carpet.

Scoots Gillespie was not only Beverlee's best friend, but also one of the nosiest people in our small beachfront town, a title she earned as a former attorney and the owner of the pawnshop that sat beneath our two apartments. People frequently came in to sell their treasured possessions and told her their saddest stories, which she shared with everyone else, claiming there is no right to privacy if you'd reveal your personal business to a stranger.

Since our viewing of *Romance Revival* included snacks and airing other people's dirty laundry, they were both insistent on joining us for the party. Wherever plentiful food and juicy gossip lived, Scoots and Beverlee were sure to be close by.

Beverlee stopped in front of the coffee table to unload enough snacks for a week. First out was a fresh baguette that I snatched before it even hit the surface.

She whirled, her hand on her hip. "Were you raised in a barn?" She lifted a brow and plucked the bread from my grip, pulling off a small hunk to toss me before depositing the rest on the tray. "No. No, you were not. I raised you in a perfectly respectable bungalow with perfectly respectable manners."

I grinned and popped the crusty end into my mouth.

Just then, Scoots strode through the door. She dropped a plastic grocery bag on the floor next to the table, then sat down on the sofa with a thunk. "I brought a can of wine and a box of hot sauce sardines somebody left in the bottom of a briefcase I acquired this afternoon. Did I miss anything?"

I grabbed the rest of the baguette and waved it toward Josie before breaking off another large piece. "Our friendly neighborhood criminal was just about to tell us how her ex-husband, love of her life and former resident of the North Carolina penal system, has turned himself into a reality star."

All eyes swung to Josie, who sat transfixed in front of the television.

"Let me get this straight," Scoots said, studying the screen. "That man, the one with the big muscles and the wavy blond hair, was your husband?"

Josie's chin dropped to her chest. "No, the other one."

Scoots reclined onto the sofa cushion, her forehead wrinkled in confusion. "The man who looks like he should be selling vacuum cleaners to retirees?"

"William Beauregard Lyons, the third," Josie replied with a stiff nod. "But everybody called him Beau."

She was still gawking at the television. "But he's... And you're... Can someone explain this to me? Is he at least rich?"

Beverlee finished arranging a platter of cookies. "Leave her alone, Scoots. Sometimes the heart is blind."

And Beverlee would know. She had been married three times and engaged a fourth. She was the grande dame of romance gone awry.

I raised the plate from the table and held it in front of Josie. "Talk," I instructed. "Did they tell you he was getting out?"

She shook her head and chose a chocolate chunk cookie. "No. The last I heard, he was in prison." She wiggled her ankle. "But to be fair, I don't get out much."

We sat for a moment, alternately shoveling food into our mouths and watching Josie gape at the sight of her husband center-stage, courting another woman.

On camera, Beau settled across the table from Lily Page, his lips curled up in a watery smile. He dragged his hand over the length of her arm, finally reaching up to cup her cheek.

At the sound of a low moan, we all swiveled toward Josie. Cookie crumbs rained down on the carpet in front of her as her hands contracted into tight fists.

"Beauregard Lyons will regret the day he sent me to jail and broke my heart," she said with a scowl. "Because I'm going to kill him."

2

That Sunday morning, I stood outside a nondescript building in the center of the Flat Falls waterfront district, trying not to throw up my breakfast. Nothing made a better first impression on a new client than a second shot at freshly swallowed avocado toast.

What had once been an area of industrial warehouses and fish canneries now harbored a charming row of bistros and ritzy gift shops targeted toward the rich tourists who liked to spend their summers on the North Carolina coast.

The warehouse, long abandoned and misused, stood as a last remnant of the shipping town before investors realized there was more money in the country club set than there would ever be in shrimp. It stretched a full city block in the space between the water and the street, weathered wood and rusted metal highlighting its slow slide into dilapidation.

When I was a teenager, though, the corroded signs that read Do Not Enter served as invitations to push aside the squeaky vent covers and sneak inside to hang out with friends or skip school.

"I'd better not catch you in there, young lady," Beverlee

told me more than once when I came tearing in the house seconds before curfew. "It's dirty and filled with unsavory characters. You could get Typhoid. Or worse, pregnant."

I shielded my eyes from the sun and took in the building now. Even though the sheets of plywood that once lined the windows had been removed, and the trim sported a fresh coat of paint, it still looked like it might require antibiotics to visit.

Seagulls flitted about overhead, and my fingers curled around a caramel latte from the Grind and Go down the street. I shifted back and forth on my heels as I peeked at my watch for the twentieth time. Whenever a vehicle slowed down on the other side of the small parking lot, I pasted on a cheerful smile.

Finally, a silver sports car squealed to a stop next to the main entrance, and a woman stepped out dressed in a tailored black suit. With her straight, chin-length dark hair, enormous eyes, and bitter scowl, she resembled a cross between a ninja and an anime princess, and my posture involuntarily straightened at the sight of her.

She bordered on being overdressed for Flat Falls, but as she flicked a disapproving glance down my body, I wished I had donned something fancier than a denim shirt dress and brown crocodile flip-flops. But they were my good flip-flops, so I was doing my best.

When her gaze made it back up to my face, she pursed her lips. "Are you the wedding planner?"

I bobbed my head and held out the black leather portfolio Beverlee gave me when I returned to Flat Falls. When she didn't make a move to take it, I stuffed the folder under my armpit and extended my hand instead. "That's me. Glory Wells with Carolina Weddings."

Her brows slashed together in a frown before she reached out slowly to shake it. "Well, at least you're on time. I'm

Mimi Wakefield, the producer of *Romance Revival*." She gestured toward the warehouse. "Before I take you inside, I will need to see your signed non-disclosure agreement and footage release forms."

Coffee sloshed over my hand as I jiggled the portfolio from under my arm. I tried to find the confidentiality paperwork the studio sent over a few days earlier, but I was short a limb. I held the drink out to Mimi. "Would you mind…?"

She responded with a thin-lipped stare.

Realizing I was blowing my first legitimate job since returning to Flat Falls and opening Carolina Weddings, I deposited the cup on the curb behind me.

I shuffled through the pages of printouts and plans, finally producing the papers with a triumphant whoop. I fluttered them in the air in front of her. "Got your forms right here," I said with far more enthusiasm than I was feeling.

She took them with the tips of her fingers as if I were asking her to hold my used chewing gum. She dropped them inside her patent leather tote bag, wiped her hand on her pants, and spun toward the warehouse. "Okay, then. Follow me."

She was already through the entrance before I remembered I'd left my coffee on the side of the street, so not only was I awkward and underdressed, but I was also a litterbug.

An icy blast hit me in the face as I followed her through the door. At least the air conditioner worked. Late fall in North Carolina still felt like walking into Satan's armpit, so a touch of cool air was always welcome.

Immediately to the side of the entrance, an enormous arrangement of fresh flowers partially hid the woman sitting behind an oversized wooden desk. "Check in here whenever you arrive," Mimi said, swishing her hand over the guest log.

"She will provide you with the proper credentials while you're on set."

I tried to give the receptionist a warm greeting as I passed by, but she didn't make eye contact. And since Mimi had taken off at a high speed toward the center of the building, I practically had to gallop down the hall to keep up with her, my flip-flops smacking on the scarred concrete floors.

Mimi bypassed the craft services table piled with muffins and fresh fruit, then came to an abrupt stop when we rounded a corner into an area crowded with people and gear. She twisted toward me with her finger pressed to her mouth.

If I squinted around the cameras and lights and ignored the dozen strangers manning pieces of equipment I had never seen, the set could pass for somebody's living room. An intricate pulley system suspended an oversized chandelier with cascading teardrop crystals over a salmon-colored velvet sofa, and modern art dotted the wood-paneled walls. Fake windows were lit from behind by large, fabric-covered light boxes.

Two cups of coffee and a plate of finger sandwiches rested untouched on a glass coffee table, and multiple cameras perched around the periphery focused on a couple engaged in conversation.

I recognized Lily, the studio lights reflecting off her shiny blond hair. The man had his back to me, so I couldn't see his face. He had hair the color of the dishwater after I'd washed a greasy pan, and he was wearing a dark polo and khaki pants, a brown-loafered foot kicked up on his opposite knee as he tilted toward his companion.

The couple carried on an animated discussion, and I was so engrossed in feeling like a voyeur I jumped when the director's booming voice came out of nowhere. "Stop. Nobody wants to hear about how you got your heart broken at summer camp. I liked the story about your daddy issues, though. So, try again, but give me more of that."

The man on the sofa turned in my direction. Sharp, bird-like eyes met mine, and a languid smile slithered across his face.

Beau. Josie's ex-husband.

Interest flashed across his face, and he raised his hand toward the cameraman. "Can we take a break for a few minutes?"

Several people murmured in agreement, and Beau stood up from the couch. He didn't even acknowledge Lily. Instead, he looped his thumbs through his belt loops, thrust his chin in the air, and headed straight for me.

When he got close enough for me to smell his breath mint, he stuck out his arm. "Beau Lyons, reality star. And you are?"

Disgusted. But I forced a polite acknowledgement and took his reptilian hand in mine. "Glory Wells, wedding planner."

His eyes crinkled at the corners, and his chest puffed out. He pressed his mouth to the inside of my wrist, and I felt my pulse thump against his chilly lips. "Ah, so you're here to make my every dream come true?"

I wrenched my palm free and fought the urge to search for the closest bottle of hand sanitizer.

Beau didn't notice my revulsion. Instead, he popped another mint, winked, and walked off the set with a stilted swagger.

I found Mimi examining me with squinted eyes. "Don't get involved with the cast."

"Wasn't planning to," I replied. *At least not with that guy.* "Is he one of the finalists?"

She looked down at her clipboard. "Yes. We've narrowed

it down to two couples. You were just watching Beau and Lily. Jason and Hazel are shooting off-site today."

I pulled out my portfolio. "Your assistant told me you're in a bit of a time crunch. She said the goal is to plan a simple ceremony to take place on the same day as the engagement shoot. Is that correct?"

"Mostly. But I've added a few extra things to the list to make the episode picture-perfect for the camera. No big deal —just flowers, cake, coordinated paper goods. Maybe a band." She plucked a pen from her jacket pocket and tapped it on her watch. "And we'll need them ready a week from Friday."

A fresh burst of panic made my fingers twitch, and my nails dug into the portfolio's cool leather. Pulling together a fake wedding in two weeks was one thing, but anything more would require a matrimonial miracle. I tried to slow my breaths so I didn't hyperventilate in front of my client. "Do you need an officiant?"

"The show's host, Javier McMasters, went to a seminar in Vegas last summer, so that's already taken care of." She flipped through a stack of papers on her clipboard and extracted two. "Here's what we would like and a shot list for you to use in your planning."

I scanned the list and blinked. Then swallowed. Then blinked again. "You want a full wedding," I stammered, my gaze shifting down the page to ensure I wasn't imagining things. "Including a seven-tier cake and an ice sculpture replica of the Eiffel Tower, in less than two weeks?"

Mimi raised brows so dark and thin they appeared drawn on with a Sharpie. "Is that a problem? If so, I'm certain there's another wedding planner in this town who would be happy to handle it for me. Think of all the publicity."

A wave of nausea rolled through me. I couldn't think of the publicity. I could only think of Magnolia Winters, the only other wedding planner in Flat Falls. Maggie had been tormenting me since I was in elementary school, and I would rather stab myself in the eye with a dirty shrimp fork than let her have this victory, despite Mimi's ridiculously obscene timeline.

"No problem at all," I replied, dread pooling in my stomach.

I would succeed with this wedding, no matter how much trouble it caused me. I couldn't let my first job with Carolina Weddings end in failure.

～

OUR LAST STOP on Mimi's whirlwind tour of the studio was the threshold to her office. "Stay here," she said, closing the door in my face.

A few minutes later, she returned carrying a folded beach towel embroidered with a yellow sea turtle and a silhouette of the Flat Falls water tower.

Some cities had award-winning skyscrapers or Andrew Lloyd Wright-designed homes. Flat Falls boasted a statue of a pig named Earl and a shiny red water tower hand-painted by the mayor's party-boy son to resemble an enormous crab pot. But since he was more than likely still drunk when he painted it, the black lines were crooked, and the result was less like its intended subject and more like Spiderman had crashed into it at top speed after a bender.

"I picked this up at the gift shop across the street," she said, holding the towel out to me.

I took it between my hands, its cheap fibers scratching my fingertips. "Thanks for the present."

"It's not a gift." She contemplated me with open scrutiny. "But you appear unprepared for the day ahead, and you Southerners love to be neighborly. I'm letting you borrow it for this morning's shoot, but please return it this afternoon. Washed, but not starched, if possible."

I considered her suggestion that people out there starched their towels. "What are we doing this—"

"We're filming Beau and Lily's last date, and we need footage of you gathering information about their ideal wedding." She pointed toward the warehouse entrance and made a shooing motion. "Get to the docks, Ms. Wells. They left ten minutes ago."

I hurried out the door and made it to the Flat Falls docks in less than five minutes. When I arrived, a crew of about ten people stood on the back of a commercial parasailing boat.

Anxiety threaded its way through my body. I had never been parasailing before, but I believed if people were meant to fly behind speed boats strapped to parachutes, we would already have wings.

Lily, outfitted in a harness and bubblegum pink life jacket, bounded off the boat and tucked her arm through mine. "You're the wedding planner, right? Come on, we'll have fun. I can't wait to hear your ideas for our ceremony."

A cameraman came around to the side of us, rolling his hand in the air to show he was filming.

Lily led me toward the boat, a sly smile showing she knew I wouldn't back out on camera.

When I stepped aboard, she motioned to a cooler strapped to the boat's deck. "Can I get you something to drink before we go?"

I shook my head, trying to figure out the charming, farm-fresh woman in front of me. With light makeup and her rosy cheeks stippled with freckles, she looked more like the star of a milk commercial than a conniving socialite with a fondness for devouring men's souls.

But before I could make sense of it, Beau strolled toward us, eyeballing me from head to toe. He seized Lily's hand and brought it to his chest before guiding her to the bench lining the boat's stern.

"We have a few minutes before we get started," I said, pretending to rifle through my notes. "So why don't you both tell me what you envision for your special day?"

Beau directed a brief smile at Lily. "I'm afraid I won't be much help in that department."

"No?" I asked, failing to hide a smug snicker. "But it says here you were married once before. Did you help your wife plan that wedding?"

He ran his fingers through his hair, surveying the water with a disinterested glance. "It was a long time ago. Things were different then."

"How so? You're young. It can't have been that long ago."

My quick math pegged Beau and Josie's wedding date at almost six years before. Long enough for him to lose track of minute details, but not so long that he'd forget everything.

Beau shifted on the bench and twisted his neck so he was facing away from Lily. "Don't you think it's disrespectful to bring up my past in front of the woman who could very well be my future?"

Romance Revival was a reality show based on flaunting its contestants' failures. I had no doubt a team in a production room somewhere had already dug up dirt on his misdeeds, including every innocent bride he'd ever sent to jail. I pinched the bridge of my nose to keep from rolling my eyes and turned to Lily, who was sitting with her hands folded in her lap. "Why don't you tell me about your dream wedding?"

Lily beamed and squeezed Beau's hand. "I've always wanted a big, glamorous ceremony like they have in all the bridal magazines."

I scribbled notes as she spoke. "That's it? Your only requirement is for your wedding to mimic a magazine?"

"Until the show came around, I didn't think I'd have

another chance to find true love." She rested her head on Beau's shoulder, her cheek pressed into his yellow life jacket. "But after the… incident, the producers contacted me and said what I needed was to believe in myself enough to grab my fresh start."

Her eyes glittered with unshed tears. "And they were right. I made a mistake, but it doesn't define me. And now I'm about to find out if I get to marry the man of my dreams."

I resisted the desire to spin around and see if a Hemsworth brother had landed on the boat as we cruised away from the dock, because I had a hard time imagining Beau Lyons as anybody's fantasy man.

"Cut," a voice from behind me boomed. "She needs a makeup refresh before they go up."

A woman with a tackle box filled with cosmetics scurried past me, patting Lily's face with a fluffy powder brush before sending her to the stern to get strapped into her harness.

When a current of air lifted Beau and Lily off the boat, the sun glinted off their red and navy parachute, and their joyful squeals sounded over the water. If I squinted and ignored the doubt ringing like a gong in my brain, they almost appeared to be a normal, happy couple.

They floated behind us for ten minutes, Lily's foot wound around Beau's ankle. From their animated gestures as they viewed the world below, the date was a success.

The captain turned on the motorized winch to reel them back to the boat, and when her feet returned to the deck, Lily grinned at me. "You're up."

I glanced over my shoulder to find a bulky black camera aimed at my face, so I took a deep breath and stepped forward. Although I had little interest in whizzing through the air high above the ocean, I really didn't want to look like a chicken on national television. "Great," I replied, offering a falsely cheerful thumbs-up.

A deckhand clipped me into a neon orange life vest, yanking the straps so tight my nostrils practically rested on my cleavage. Sea spray misted my legs as I shivered on the platform waiting to take off into the sky with only a thin rope standing between me and a video crew ready to televise my gruesome demise.

When the parachute filled with air and lifted me off the deck, I stifled a scream to keep the small camera mounted to an extension pole on the crossbar in front of me from capturing footage of my exposed tonsils.

When I didn't plunge to my death after several minutes of white-knuckling the harness, I began to relax. Flat Falls was picturesque from the ground, but absolutely stunning from five hundred feet above the shoreline. Long rows of colorful houses lined the streets, and tiny dots of color I assumed were people lounged on the beach and played in the surf.

The sun shimmered on the water, and a smile tugged at my lips as I enjoyed the peaceful breeze and the steady hum of the boat's engine.

My heartbeat had just returned to normal when the harness tugged against my back, signaling the start of my return to firm ground.

My descent slowed midway to the boat, and the crew scrambled to adjust the winch, motioning to me with sweeping arms. Their frenzied shouts vanished in the air as blood pumped through my ears at breakneck speed.

Suddenly, the rope went slack, and I hurtled toward the water, landing with a violent gurgle in a tangle of brightly colored nylon and twisted rope.

I sputtered, salty ocean water filling my mouth, as they manually pulled in the line. When I finally reached the boat, the captain towed me out of the waves and deposited me like a bloated swordfish in the center of the deck.

"Sorry about that," he muttered, casting an apologetic glance over my waterlogged denim dress. "The winch got stuck."

My throat burned from the saltwater, and my skin was peppered with goosebumps. I swiped the back of my hand across my cheek and grimaced at the streak of mascara. But the camera was still recording, so I gave a jaunty wave instead of flipping off the crew. "It was a nice day for a swim."

Mimi was waiting for us under a black umbrella when we returned to the dock. With eyes hidden behind oversized sunglasses, she resembled a demented Mary Poppins.

She cleared her throat as I climbed off the boat. "My towel?"

I squeezed my dripping hair with the cloth before releasing it onto her outstretched palm and stepping around her.

Just before I passed, her arm shot out and locked on my wrist. "Remember, you signed a confidentiality agreement. I know this is a small town, but you can't tell anyone what happens during filming."

∼

"Tell me everything," Josie ordered as I settled onto her sofa later that afternoon.

I shook my head. "Sorry, I can't. Top secret." I pretended to zip my lips shut, but then she held out a shortbread cookie, and I had to unzip them to shove it in.

"Did you see him?"

"Who, Beau?" I asked, fully aware of who she was talking about, but not wanting to discuss her creeper ex.

She scowled and grabbed hold of the cookie. "I will stop baking you treats unless you tell me what I want to know."

As far as threats went, it was a significant one. Josie didn't have much else to do, so she regularly supplied me with baked goods. She was my dealer, and I wasn't about to cut off my supply.

I exhaled and yanked it from her grip, then took a big bite. Crumbs fell across the front of my shirt as I replied with my mouth full. "Fine. Yes, I saw him."

"And?"

"And what? He was in the middle of shooting. I couldn't exactly interrogate him."

She pushed up her sleeves with two quick jerks. "What kind of scene was it?"

"I can't tell you that!"

"Well, you confirmed that he's here in Flat Falls, so I know he made it past the first few rounds."

"I really can't..."

Josie continued. "And because you're there planning a wedding, I have to assume he's made it almost to the finale. The research I found online said that *Romance Revival* was only supposed to film through the end of October, which is in two weeks."

I grabbed another cookie to keep from having to respond.

Josie leaned back and extended a finger. "So you're telling me Beau is a finalist, and he's going to marry somebody else in two weeks. Somebody that isn't me."

I sat up straighter. "What? I didn't..."

She tilted toward me, her face less than a foot from mine. "Who is she?"

"Like I said, I can't tell you." I pressed my thumbs into my eyebrows to ward off the headache building behind my eyes.

"It's that big-chested woman from Boise, isn't it? The one who got famous on YouTube for participating in those hot dog eating contests in a string bikini top?"

I dropped my head into my hands. "No, it's not her."

"Then who? Who is marrying my husband?" She paced through the room like a caged animal. And since her house arrest meant she basically was a caged animal, her anxiety was contagious. "Is it the one who carries around the hedgehog in her pocket?"

"Why does it really matter, Jo?" I spoke in my most calming voice, the voice of reason I usually reserved for Beverlee when I was trying to talk her out of something like naked skydiving or getting married again. "He's your ex-husband. Ex. You're not together anymore."

She ignored me and walked back and forth in front of the sofa tapping her fingers against each other like a human praying mantis, all long, thin limbs and entwined hands. She finally stopped and stared down at me. "Please tell me it wasn't the pickle princess."

I didn't respond, and she immediately took it as an affirmation that Beau was, indeed, planning to marry Lily Page.

"Are you kidding me? The pickle lady?" Josie shrieked.

She plopped down on the sofa next to me with a feral whine and hauled the entire plate of cookies into her lap. She began shoveling them into her mouth, pushing a new one in before she had even finished chewing the old one. Her eyes were wild, her long hair a mass of frizz like deflated cotton candy.

"Mainlining shortbread won't help." I put my hand on the plate to confiscate it, but Josie batted my fingers away. I gazed at the kitchen wistfully. "But if you really want to do some damage, maybe you could try double chocolate chip."

With a defiant glare, she seized another cookie and held it to her chest. But after a few moments, her destructive chewing slowed, and she blinked up at me. "You're right. But I need to talk to him. I need to find out why he did it. Why he broke my heart, and why he let me take the blame for something I didn't have any part in." Josie wiggled her ankle to remind me of how much she had lost.

This, I understood. After my ex-husband stole the auction cash box from my last paying job as an event planner back in Raleigh, then hightailed it out of town with my money and my heart, I would have given anything for the chance to confront him.

Too bad he disappeared. Not even the private investigator I hired had been able to pin him down.

"I get it," I said. "But I don't see how I can help you. They won't let you in to talk to him. They have security all around the warehouse to keep out the fans." I pointed to her foot. "And besides, you're not allowed to leave the house."

She picked up her laptop, then after a few moments turned the screen to face me. "This warehouse? The empty one down on the waterfront?"

Since I had already broken the confidentiality agreement, I took a deep breath and said, "It's the only space big enough to handle the show's gear."

Josie nodded, but I could tell her mind was elsewhere. "Do you think you could get a message to him? Can you tell him I need to talk to him?"

"That's not a good idea. I'm only there to plan the wedding."

I reached out to take the last cookie, but Josie pulled the plate toward her with a protective snarl.

"As much as I want to help you find closure, I can't mess up this opportunity by going stalker-fan on a potential groom," I said. "And besides, it's not like I get one-on-one access to the contestants."

She pursed her lips and continued to hold the cookies hostage.

Trying to soften the blow of words no heartbroken woman wants to hear, I gave her an apologetic smile. "Josie, maybe it's time you moved on."

Her eyes flashed in anger as she picked up the cookie. "I'll move on once I've dealt with Beau."

∼

LATER THAT NIGHT, Mimi made Josie's wish come true in a way neither one of us could have planned.

After I left Josie cuddled up with a bottle of Tums and a promise to lay off the cookies, I returned to my apartment to flip through Mimi's hand-written wedding wish list.

I was pondering how to come up with a live orchestra and a marshmallow fluff fountain when a loud bang from the porch made me jump. I pressed my face to the peephole to find a man with fists resembling corned hams banging against Josie's wooden door. A second man lingered on the top step with something large and black resting on his shoulder, like a boom box or a rocket launcher.

Since Josie and I occupied the only two apartments above the pawnshop, and I assumed neither one of us had ordered delivery of a giant weapon, I threw the door open and stepped out onto the porch with an impatient sigh. "Can I help you?" I demanded.

The banging stopped, and they pivoted to look at my door. Mimi cruised out of the shadows holding a microphone, and the beefcake from the stairs inched forward, lugging what turned out to be a shoulder-mounted camera.

"Oh, it's you. The wedding planning lady," Mimi said sweetly, and I knew she couldn't remember my name.

"Glory Wells," I reminded her.

28

I inclined my head toward the lens, saying a silent prayer of thanks that I hadn't greeted them in my pajamas.

Mimi ignored my statement and moved in, a slow smile spreading across her face. "We're looking for Josie."

"I'm right here," Josie said, the door creaking as she pulled off her earbuds and stepped out onto the porch.

She was wearing a spandex sports bra printed with fireworks and a pair of stretchy black leggings, and with her flushed cheeks and sweat-dampened curls, I could tell she had been doing yoga.

The cameraman stared at her exposed belly ring until Mimi cleared her throat and jerked her head toward Josie's face.

"We didn't mean to come by uninvited," Mimi said. "But your number was unlisted, and we wanted to give you a chance to speak up before the finale."

"Speak up?" Josie asked, her forehead wrinkling in confusion. "About what?"

Mimi stepped back until she hit the rusty aluminum porch rail. Behind her, in the alley between the bank and the water, Beau Lyons stood with his hands shoved in his pockets.

For the first time, I noticed a second camera crew positioned at the bottom of the stairs, positioned for a wide-angle view of the meeting between Josie and the man who sent her to jail.

She gasped and whirled to face me.

I held my palms up in the air, wanting her to know I had nothing to do with this impromptu gathering. "Not me."

"Beau?" Josie stepped forward, confusion wrinkling her brow.

"Surely there are things you want to say to him," Mimi interjected.

Josie glanced at Beau, then back at Mimi. "Right now?"

"Is there a better time to tell him how you feel? All that heartache. All those tears. Don't you need him to answer for breaking your heart?"

Mimi slipped her hand out behind her and a production assistant lurched forward with her clipboard. "All you need to do is sign this release form."

A warning pinged through my head. I crossed the porch to Josie's side, clamping my hand on her shoulder. "I don't think that's a good idea."

Mimi thrust the clipboard toward her chest. "I'll throw in a thousand dollars for your trouble."

"That's bribery," I said.

"It's show business," she countered, her lips pursed and her foot tapping on the metal floor.

Josie grabbed the clipboard and scribbled her name across the form without even reading it, then turned to me with a shrug. "It might be my only chance."

Mimi positioned herself in front of the camera and cleared her throat. "We recently discovered that the young woman who played an important role in Beau's downward criminal spiral, his first wife, lives right here in Flat Falls." She paused, her right eyebrow arched toward the water-stained ceiling. "At *Romance Revival*, we don't believe in coincidences. Let's see what happens when two former lovers meet again for the first time in several years."

I dipped my chin, ignoring the sense of dread building in my chest. I could already tell this meeting wouldn't end well, but there was no way I'd get between Josie and her opportunity for closure.

Josie straightened her spine and stepped around the camera, stopping at the top of the stairs to face Beau.

He pulled his hand from his pocket and lifted it in a wave. "Hey, babe," he said. "You look good."

"That's where you start?" Josie's response was measured. "Not *I'm sorry* or *I was wrong*, but 'You look good?'"

She took the stairs slowly, but without hesitation. She had gone from victim to predator, and I felt a bit sorry for him. From his loose stance, one of his hands still tucked into his pocket, Beau did not anticipate the wrath she was about to unleash on him.

The rest of us did, though.

Mimi bounced on the tips of her toes as she watched, and I held my breath as the cameraman zoomed in on Josie's flushed face.

"You sent me to jail." Her jaw clenched, and indignation blazed in her eyes. "You knew those were ghost employees you had me set up on the payroll."

Beau's shoulders caved. "Josie, I can explain."

"Explain?" she roared. "There is no explanation. You used me to divert company funds into accounts for people who *did not even exist*. And then you pocketed the money."

He flinched. "I'm sorry, Jo, I'm so—"

Josie's fingers flexed on the bottom porch rail, and before I could stop her, she launched herself across the alley and headed straight for him. The slap of her palm crossing his cheek echoed over the water, but it was nothing compared to the screeches she unleashed as she pounded her fists into his chest.

"How could you do this to me?" she screamed. "I loved you, and you used me—"

"Josie, stop." He grabbed her arms and cast a frantic look at the closest cameraman, but nobody stepped in to help. Instead, the *Romance Revival* team circled the couple like they were cheering for a boxing match, no doubt capturing the spectacle from multiple angles.

"Stop?" She yanked her hands free and reared back to

shove him so hard he stumbled against the force. "You want me to stop? I won't stop until you've paid for what you did."

I elbowed my way between Mimi and a sound tech. I held one hand up to the camera like a shield and wrapped the other around Josie's upper arm, giving it a firm tug. "That didn't go how you envisioned, did it?"

As I hauled her up the stairs, still letting off years of pent-up hostility, I glanced at Mimi, noting her undisguised bliss as she watched the scene unfold. In less than five minutes, Josie had given her enough footage to turn *Romance Revival*'s leading contestant from a sniveling pencil pusher into a heartbroken victim.

3

I spent the next morning fielding messages from Mimi, each one adding a layer of complexity to an already complicated ceremony. Every time I thought she had finished making her wish list, she'd add something else, and what started as simple set decoration quickly became "the biggest wedding television has ever seen."

At just after three o'clock, when I had finally put away the stacks of papers and pads of sticky notes and sat down with a reheated slice of pepperoni pizza, my phone rang.

"We're about to wrap for a late lunch," Mimi said. "And I have a few minor details I'd like to go over with you in person. Can you be here in twenty minutes?"

I peeked down at my ratty sweats and the greasy plate and sighed. "Of course," I replied between gritted teeth. "I'd be happy to."

However, when I parked in front of the warehouse, I didn't find the line of fans and paparazzi I was expecting. Instead, a horde of confused onlookers milled around behind a boundary of yellow police tape, and bright red lights flashed sharply on the warehouse's metal walls. It looked like they were filming in the middle of a zombie disco instead of a quaint Southern coastal town.

I spotted Hollis Goodnight, chief of the Flat Falls police department, next to the front door. When he saw me, he scrubbed his hand along his scalp. "Glory Wells, please tell me you were in the neighborhood and you had nothing to do with this."

His gray hair was standing on end, a sign he had already reached his frustration threshold. I had walked that line with him more often than I cared to admit, and his hair stuck straight out for most of my teenage years.

"Not me," I said, glancing between him and the people gathering outside the warehouse. "What happened?"

Just then, Mimi pushed the door open, letting it hit the metal wall with a clang that reverberated around the parking lot. She scanned the area, and when she spotted me, she rushed out and clutched my arm. Instead of lugging me inside, though, she guided me to an empty spot near the far corner of the building.

Over my shoulder, I saw the stunned police chief watching us with narrowed eyes. I lifted my hand and gave him a small finger waggle.

"Something came up." Mimi's breath huffed out in short pants, her eyes darting toward the emergency personnel rushing in and out of the door. "I need you to handle the wedding preparations on your own for a little while."

"Okaaaay," I said slowly, wondering what caused her to relinquish the overdeveloped sense of control that just that morning had her demanding approval rights between two almost identical shades of cream napkins. "Did something happen?"

"You could say that. We spent half an hour dealing with a photographer who was trying to sneak in past security, then we lost one of our grooms." Then she pivoted and marched back toward the building.

"Wait," I called after her. "What do you mean, you lost a groom? Which one? And how am I supposed to plan a…"

I surveyed the crowd, and by the time I decided this was not the place to break the show's confidentiality agreement, Mimi had already slipped inside. I stared after her, wondering how she expected me to coordinate a wedding with a runaway groom.

"Glory, can I talk to you for a minute?" I looked up and found the Sheriff motioning to me.

"What's up, Hollis?"

He shuffled his feet, and a blush crept up his weathered cheeks. "Listen, I planned to have dinner with Beverlee tonight. She was making chicken and dumplings." He raked his gaze over the mob with a scowl. "But I can't make it, after all."

Hollis had been in love with my aunt for as long as I could remember. She had no idea, so she continued to invite him to dinner, usually along with a random woman from town who she said would make him a splendid wife. And he dutifully attended every time, showing up with wine or flowers, while Beverlee was oblivious to his smitten glances.

I patted his arm. "I'll call her, and I'm sure she'll save you a plate."

A dark sedan pulled to a stop a few feet away from us. "Thank you," he said, his voice low and somber. "Now if you'll excuse me, the coroner is here."

Hollis turned to greet the woman that climbed out of the car.

My scalp tingled, and alarm snaked down toward my stomach as I took in the bright lights and the police presence.

Coroner?

The groom hadn't run away. He was dead.

~

I CALLED Beverlee to relay Hollis's message. When I mentioned there might be a corpse on set, she immediately whooped and said she'd meet me at the warehouse. There hadn't been much excitement in Flat Falls since the last dead body, so this gave her an excuse to put on lipstick and head out for a night on the town.

After disconnecting, I surveyed the gawkers whispering in the parking lot. As an independent contractor for the show, I had a vested interest in knowing what was going on behind those metal walls. That, and I was nosy.

There was a fifty percent chance the dead groom in question was Josie's ex-husband, so friendship rules required I get as much information as possible.

I moved toward the crowd, catching bits and pieces of their theories. Drug overdose. Romantic dispute. Alien abduction.

I wasn't sure why suspected visits from extraterrestrials always topped the list when weird things happened in this town, but aliens were unlikely on a random Tuesday in the middle of October, so I pushed my way through the throng and searched for more reliable observers. A redheaded man with a camera threw an elbow, but I flashed a smile and a quick, "I work here" and continued forward.

When I made it to a clearing near the building, I spotted Gage Russell, a former high school classmate who now wore a Flat Falls Police badge pinned to his well-muscled chest. I gave a weak wave. "I hear you've got a dead guy."

"Hello to you, too, Glory," he responded with a lifted brow. "And where did you hear that?"

"Everybody knows, Gage. Don't play coy." I tipped my chin toward the door. "Can you tell me who it was?"

"All I've heard is they were filming something, there was a loud bang, and a big chandelier fell on an actor's head. Took him right out."

I scanned over my shoulder to make sure nobody was listening and whispered, "What did he look like? Brown hair, sort of nerdy?"

A vein throbbed in his neck. "He looked like a man pancaked in a Looney Tunes cartoon, if you want the truth."

Frustrated, I dangled my secret weapon. "Gage, you've met Josie, right?"

I already knew the answer to that. Gage had been sniffing around Josie for the last few months under the guise of welfare checks. But making googly eyes at a criminal when you delivered takeout to her apartment after your shift every Wednesday didn't normally fall under official jurisdiction.

His eyes flicked to me with interest. "What does she have to do with this?"

"Mimi, the producer, said a groom died." I pointed toward the warehouse, then bent in so only he could hear me. "One of those grooms was Josie's ex-husband."

"The same ex-husband that had her thrown in jail?"

"That's him."

"The one who is responsible for her being on house arrest?" he asked, his expression hardening.

"Yep."

He crossed his arms, and a slow smile spread across his handsome face. "Now that you mention it, I believe the deceased did have brown hair."

I was about to confirm my suspicion that Beau was under that chandelier when Beverlee's yellow convertible skidded to a stop near the edge of the crowd. The horn sounded two peppy beeps, then she popped out of the driver's side.

"Glory!" she shouted as she barreled forward, greeting townspeople and strangers alike with quick hugs and big smiles as if she were walking a red carpet instead of skirting police barricades. She halted when she reached me. "What's the scoop? Is it somebody we know?"

I peeked over my shoulder at Gage, who was now speaking in hushed tones with a crew member, and bit my lip. "I'm not allowed to talk about it."

Beverlee crossed her arms and cocked her head. "Glory Ann Wells, I raised you from the time you were no bigger than a flea in a tick circus. I have changed your diapers. Don't start hiding things from me now."

I steered her to the side of the group. "Listen, you didn't hear it from me," I said. "But a chandelier fell from the ceiling and landed on a contestant."

"Which contestant?" she demanded. "What aren't you telling me?"

I sighed. "I think it was William Beauregard Lyons, the third."

Beverlee stared down at the ground and wiggled her toes like she always did when she was deep in thought. I used to wonder if she was obsessed with her pedicure, but a few years ago she told me something about her feet being connected to her brain chakra, so I let it slide. Finally, she focused on me and snapped her finger. "Isn't that…"

"Yes, it's Josie's ex-husband."

She made a sound that was part cough and part chuckle, then covered her mouth with her hand. After she regained her composure, she pulled out her cell phone. "It's a terrible shame when bad guys get what's coming to them, isn't it?"

She stepped over to a concrete wall near the edge of the parking lot and held out her arm. "Here, help me up."

I eyed the gravel lot and the four-foot divider looming

above it. "No. I've got enough to deal with. I don't have time for your broken femur."

She huffed. "I'll have you know I joined a senior rock-climbing league down at the Flat Falls YMCA."

"You did what?" I asked. "And why?"

"Ernie Kellerman invited me," she said with a grin. "And I thought if he stood underneath me as I climbed, it might be the excuse he needed to put his hands on my bottom."

"You became a rock climber to get felt up by the man who takes his teeth out and leaves them on the counter at the Grind and Go while he drinks his coffee every morning?" My jaw ached from where my molars were smashed together. "We have higher standards than that, Beverlee."

"I don't want to marry him, Glory. I just want to have a good time. Something you might consider now and then." She pinned me with a glare. "Help me up."

I groaned and gave her a boost to get on the wall, then stood nearby in case she lost her footing. Within three minutes, she had invited a strapping young production assistant to hoist her down, which he did with a friendly smile.

Once she was back on the ground, she beamed at me. "And that's how it's done."

"What?" I asked.

She flipped her phone around to show me the screen. "My blog readers like to keep up with the action in our charming town, so I snapped a few pictures of the crowd. Hollis might be able to use them as evidence, too."

Although *Beverlee's Bites* had a substantial following in Flat Falls, I doubted Hollis would require the insight of a geriatric food and party blogger to solve a crime. She might be nosy, but she wasn't Columbo.

The mob around the warehouse had continued to grow, and when the mobile video crew from the mainland cable station entered the lot in their large, flashy van, I turned to Beverlee with a frown. "Somebody needs to tell Josie before she hears about it on the news. I know there's no love lost between those two, but I can't let her be alone when she finds out Beau finally got what was coming to him."

IT WAS after dark by the time I climbed the rusty metal stairs behind the pawnshop to the porch between our apartments. The breeze carried the smell of seaweed and salty air instead of the usual decaying trash stench from the rusty dumpster that occupied the small alley between the building and the pier that lined the Intracoastal waterway.

Part of me wanted to go hide under a blanket in my living room so I didn't have to deliver bad news. But Josie was a friend. I crossed the porch and knocked softly at her apartment door instead.

She opened it, pressing a red-tinged tissue to her lips. "Did you get in another fight?" I asked.

"Who am I going to fight with around here, Glory? The dust bunnies are pretty docile."

"Then why are you bleeding?"

"I'm not. It's hibiscus mint," she said, lifting a scarlet popsicle with her other hand. "I got it from the health food store on the waterfront. Want one?"

My stomach dropped. "The shop next to the warehouse?"

She nodded, lifting her ankle and waggling it around. "I needed a reason to go down there, so I asked for permission to shop at the specialty store."

The conditions of Josie's house arrest allowed her to visit the grocery store and go to medical appointments, but any other destination required sign-off from her corrections officer. "They let you make a special trip for popsicles?"

"He thinks I'm a vegan, and I made it a point to tell him the Food Barn down the street doesn't carry heirloom walnuts or organic tofu."

"But you're not a vegan."

Josie grinned and slurped the melted syrup as it dripped down her fingers. "He doesn't know that. And besides, I just needed an excuse to be down there."

"At the warehouse?"

She dipped her chin. "I was trying to find Beau. To apologize. He's a jerk, but I shouldn't have attacked him like that. The camera crew made me think he wanted to make amends to look good on TV."

"Josie, there's something I need—"

"It was chaotic down there today, so I couldn't get through. I'll try again tomorrow when the frenzy from filming has died down." She wiped her lips with the tissue. "And the barbecue tempeh burgers the butcher ordered for me will be there, so it will definitely be worth the trip."

I shifted on my feet. "The mayhem down there wasn't because of filming. There was an accident on the set of the show today."

"The pickle princess hit a sour patch?" She snickered.

"No, that's not it." I rolled my shoulders to loosen the knot of tension that had settled in my neck. "Josie, something happened to Beau."

She swayed side to side, her brows furrowed in confusion, and the color draining from her cheeks. "My Beau?"

"Yes. A chandelier fell and landed right on him." I inhaled slowly. "I'm sorry, Jo, but he didn't make it."

"My Beau?" she repeated. "Are you sure?"

I nodded.

She dropped her head into her hands, and her shoulders trembled. I had always been awkward around grief, but I wanted to comfort her, so I reached over and patted her gently on the arm. "Hollis and Gage are down at the warehouse trying to figure out exactly what happened."

Josie lifted her chin, and I realized her shoulders weren't shaking because I upset her. She was laughing. She dabbed the corner of her eye with her dirty tissue.

"Oh, I know what happened," she said, a knowing smile flitting across her lips. "Karma."

4

I left Josie and her dead ex-husband afterglow and headed to my apartment. Even though the sky had darkened, and shadows covered the porch, I could still make out a lump of fur curled up on the worn straw doormat.

"Hey, Rusty," I greeted the golden retriever.

Although he belonged to Ian Strickland, my once-upon-a-time, Rusty was our neighborhood mascot and had been visiting me every evening since I returned to town. I wasn't sure if he was lonely because Ian worked nights at Trolls, the bar he owned, or if he just recognized me as the sucker who shared her dinner with him. Either way, I was thankful for the company.

I eyed Ian's boat as it rocked gently under the glow of a full moon. I still couldn't believe we were neighbors. I could stand on the porch and toss rocks across the alley at his boat, and if I had a better arm, I'd probably hit it. I was practically living in his lap, a thought that made me more than a little warm.

The boat's on-board lights were off, and I released the breath I had been holding. Seeing him brought back feelings

I wasn't ready to face, and although Ian still hadn't forgiven me for leaving town after high school and breaking his heart, he had been surprisingly kind in welcoming me home.

Rusty didn't open his eyes as I rummaged through my purse for my keys. But from the rhythmic thump of his tail on the mat, he knew I was there.

I reached across him to unlock the door. Ever the gentleman, he waited for me to high-step over his sturdy body before getting up, retrieving his favorite pink tennis ball with his teeth, and lumbering into my foyer.

He dropped the ball from his jowls onto my ottoman before sliding back down to the floor with a groan. I nudged it off with my knee. "Thanks for thinking of me, buddy, but you can keep your slimy balls to yourself."

The ball fell to the ground with a splat, then rolled across the room. Rusty studied it with one eye open. After he decided it wasn't worth the chase, he watched me walk into the kitchen, tug open a cabinet, and pull out two cans of soup and a sleeve of crackers. "We've got chicken noodle and split pea. What'll it be?"

Rusty let out a high-pitched yawp and jumped up to follow me. He focused on the cans, then on me, finally sounding off another quick bark.

"Fine," I said. "Split pea it is. But I can't avoid poultry forever because you have a crush on Matilda."

Matilda was Beverlee's prized chicken and was the closest thing I'd ever had to a sister.

Sibling rivalry was complicated, especially when you're sharing affection with poultry, but Beverlee took her role as Matilda's caretaker every bit as seriously as she had when I was dumped on her doorstep at age five. She parented with love and baked goods, and we were both lucky she had rescued us.

Being an actual human didn't make me the favorite,

though. I got my hand slapped the week before when I tried to steal a pumpkin sugar cookie from the cooling rack in Beverlee's kitchen. "Those are for Matilda," she shrieked.

She had even knitted Matilda a bright red cabled chicken sweater to keep her warm during the upcoming Carolina winter. She'd never made me a sweater.

The chicken had everybody fooled. Even the dog, it seemed.

I heated the soup in the microwave and opened the crackers. I was about to sit down and enjoy my evening ritual of fine dining with a hundred-pound beefcake when a soft knock had Rusty on his feet announcing a new arrival with a series of short, sharp barks. With a sigh, I crossed to the door, expecting that Josie had finally come to her senses and was here to freak out about her ex-husband's death.

Instead, Ian leaned against the doorframe, slightly disheveled in faded jeans and a wrinkled black t-shirt.

He glanced through the pass-through at the can of soup on the counter and cocked an eyebrow. "If I had known you were eating dog food for dinner, I'd have brought over some wings."

My stomach growled, and I peeked at the clock. "Why aren't you at work?"

"They had the area down by the waterfront closed because some guy died."

He pointed toward the floor, where Rusty was happily licking the now-empty sleeve of crackers. "I was wondering if you had my dog."

I glared at Rusty. "I said I'd share my dinner, not that you could eat it all. You're a cracker hog."

Ian chuckled. "He's also a bed hog."

"I wouldn't know. These days, he only uses me for my food."

Ian raked a slow gaze over me. "Then he's doing it wrong."

My cheeks burned. The boy who once held my heart had turned into a man capable of making my stomach flip around like it was in the middle of a Category 5 hurricane.

Ian snapped his fingers, and Rusty jumped to attention. He pointed toward the door. "Out. You're grounded, remember?"

Rusty made a show of dropping his pouty face to the floor at Ian's feet.

I bent down and rubbed his soft, floppy ear. "Oh, no. What did you do this time?"

Ian glared at the dog, but the corner of his mouth curved up in a smile, so I knew Rusty wasn't in that much trouble. "He brought me a present earlier."

I scratched Rusty under the chin. "Who's a good boy?" I asked.

"Not him," Ian replied with a quick shake of his head. "It was a dead fish, and he left it on top of me. In my bed."

"Now that you mention it, your new cologne is hard to miss," I said, waving my hand in front of my nose. Although he didn't smell like fish guts, I enjoyed the old pattern of teasing him and watching the dimple flash in his cheek.

"You grew up here, same as me. Can't be the first time somebody fish-flopped you." I slid the living room curtain aside and studied the early evening sun as it faded over the water. "And what were you doing in bed, anyway? It's not even dark outside."

He ran his fingers through his hair. "I had a late night yesterday and was trying to catch a bit of sleep before heading back into the bar."

"What kind of late night?" I tried to sound nonchalant, but I wasn't ready to hear about Ian's love life.

"Bigwigs from some reality show are in town. They said

the time change hadn't hit them yet, so they were still raring to go when I shoved them out the door at three this morning. Can't complain, though. You wouldn't believe the cash they dropped on appetizers and drinks, even while they were arguing about how small their budget is. It seems like Hollywood's pockets run deeper than its common sense."

"They're going to need some money to get out of this mess," I said, my heart pounding at the thought of losing my inaugural client. "They can't continue filming with a deceased star."

Ian rocked back on his heels and regarded me with amusement. "Why are you always the first one to know about dead guys?"

I lifted a shoulder. "I'm sort of working with the show now."

"The reality show?" he asked.

I nodded. "But my brush with fame might be short-lived, because without their star, there is no *Romance Revival*."

AFTER IAN AND RUSTY LEFT, I opened another sleeve of crackers and fell asleep on the sofa watching Food Network reruns, only to be awakened an hour later by the sound of heavy footsteps on the metal stairs outside.

I brushed the crumbs off my shirt and tugged open the door to find the *Romance Revival* crew reprising their roles as Josie's tormenters.

Mimi stepped forward in a black pantsuit, the satin lapels reflecting the light from a portable softbox angled toward her from the top of the stairs. Her short bob was slicked back, and she fiddled with a brooch that resembled a gemstone-encrusted serpent. "Good evening, Ms. Walton."

"It's Wells," I replied, inclining my head toward the camera. "Seems late to be recording, don't you think?"

Mimi turned in slow motion, an indulgent smile spreading across her face. "A terrible tragedy has befallen one of our own tonight," she began, her voice low and measured like she was voicing a movie trailer. "Beau Lyons was once an upstanding member of North Carolina society. And he made a mistake." She gave a dramatic pause. "One that ultimately cost him his life."

I snorted and leaned against the doorframe. "He was a criminal, that part is correct. But he didn't die getting shivved in prison. He died because he got hit in the head by a light fixture." I shrugged. "Accidents happen."

"Yes, accidents *do* happen, Ms. Wells," she said with a pointed glare. "But we just uncovered shocking new information regarding Beau's past." Another long pause. "Information that could change the course of the investigation."

"Investigation?" I asked, my voice rising. "What are you talking about?"

Mimi ignored me as she prowled toward the camera.

"We recently introduced you to Beau's ex-wife, Josie Lyons, a woman with a history of abusive behavior," Mimi said. "And today, Beau Lyons is dead. We're here to uncover the truth about what actually happened to the star of *Romance Revival*. Did his wife Josie play a role in his untimely death?"

I held a finger in the air. "First, she was his ex-wife. A fact I'm sure you already grasped, or this would be a completely different television show. And second, Josie has been…"

Fate kept my fist from landing on Mimi's left cheek when Josie's door banged open, and she stepped out onto the porch. Her gaze bounced back and forth between me and

Mimi in confusion. "Glory?" she asked, blinking rapidly. "What's going on?"

She was dressed in short cutoff jeans and a tank top, her curls gathered into a messy topknot, feathery tendrils sticking out in every direction. Streaks of paint covered her skin. A bright red stripe ran down the side of her face and down toward her collarbone. It appeared an awful lot like blood. She slouched against the doorframe, a pose she often adopted when she was in the zone painting and hadn't stopped for a break in hours but which I'm sure seemed to the rest of the world like a particularly vibrant shade of crazy.

"The crew was just leaving," I said, motioning for her to head back inside.

"We were hoping to talk to you about what happened today." Mimi swiveled toward the camera and lowered her chin. "And to give you a chance to go on record about your tragic life with Beau Lyons, a story of what happens when the right love goes wrong."

"Oh, for goodness' sake." I moved to stand in front of Josie, whose glazed eyes were focused, wide and unblinking, on Mimi. "They aren't married anymore. That's why she's called an ex. There's no story here."

She shoved the microphone toward Josie. "Anything you'd like to say about your assault on the deceased? Was it a crime of passion?"

Josie pressed a fluttery palm against her chest. "I... I don't..."

"No comment," I responded, glowering at the producer.

We all stood on the porch in awkward silence until Mimi gave a decisive jerk of her head to the cameraman, who flipped off the camera before they all trekked down the steps in creepy harmony.

At the last minute, I called out to her. "See you at work tomorrow."

Mimi never looked back.

As I ushered Josie into her apartment, I spotted a lone figure in the shadow of the dumpster behind the pawnshop. I squinted and could barely make out the shock of gray hair. "Hollis, what are you doing hiding in the dark?" I motioned for him to come up.

He took the steps slowly, his eyes never leaving Josie. When he reached the landing, he stopped to ensure the video team had driven away before he finally spoke. "You handled that well, but it's a circus down at the warehouse. The show is taking full advantage of the publicity. There are news vans filled with attention-starved jackals dying to start rumors."

He motioned for both of us to go into Josie's apartment. "Can we talk where there aren't any unwanted ears?"

That seemed to jar Josie out of her stupor. She shook her head as if she were trying to clear her thoughts, then closed the door. "What's going on, Chief?"

"Those people will do anything to sniff out a story," he said, hitching his pants legs up before sitting down on the sofa. "Unfortunately, that means you two need to stay on your toes."

"What does this have to do with us?" I asked.

Hollis tilted forward, his forearms on his knees. "What happened at the warehouse this evening wasn't an accident. The evidence suggests foul play."

"Foul play?" Josie's eyes went round, and she slumped against the wall. "What does that even mean?"

Hollis tented his fingers together. "Ladies, Beau Lyons was murdered."

5

The next morning, I stood in front of my closet trying to find something that was work-appropriate for the day after a murder.

I settled on sleek charcoal cigarette pants and a pale pink silk t-shirt, then tugged on a matching cardigan.

At five minutes before nine, I knocked on the warehouse door. When nobody answered, I stalked around the exterior of the building to peek in the windows.

The glass was dark, like someone had taped dark trash bags to the inside of the panes. It was an effective way to keep out prying paparazzi. Or hide a murder.

When I turned to check another window, I stepped into a hard wall of muscled chest. A shaggy-haired security guard dressed in a black shirt and olive cargo pants reached out to steady me as I stumbled backward.

"Excuse me, miss," he said, his Southern drawl almost as thick as the humidity-drenched morning air. "This is private property. And it doesn't matter how cute you are, I will remove you if you don't leave on your own."

His wide shoulders, salon-worthy highlights, and loose

stance blended in well in a town full of beach bums and bikini babes, but the jagged scar that slashed through his left eyebrow and arched toward icy blue eyes had me scanning the area for a quick escape.

"You can't have me removed," I replied, skirting him and calculating how quickly I could make it to the door. "I work here."

He mirrored my pace as I hastened around the building. "I don't think so. I've never seen you on the set before."

"I'm the wedding planner," I said, increasing my speed. "And I'm here trying to… plan a wedding."

My breaths came quickly, and a sheen of sweat was collecting on my forehead. I added a gym membership to my mental shopping list.

The guard took two long strides and swung around to block my path.

I stopped short to avoid running into him again. "But nobody answered the door."

"That's because we were having an all-hands meeting in the back." He crossed his arms, tanned muscles flexing under his thin cotton shirt. "Which you would have known if you were actually an employee and not a reporter trying to sniff out a story where there isn't one."

I straightened my spine and tried to step around him, but his hand snaked out and tightened around my upper arm. His fingers pressed into my flesh just hard enough to transfer the threat without saying a word.

Common sense and the need for a paying job won out over my annoyance. I took a deep breath. "I'm a contractor. You can call—"

"Jimbo, let her go." Mimi stalked toward us and dismissed him with a flick of her wrist, then faced me. "It's about time you showed up."

I flashed the guard a smug grin. "Good morning, Mimi. I got here a few minutes ago, but the—"

She ignored me and spun back to the building. "Never mind. Just follow me. We have to do damage control before the wedding."

I rushed to catch up with her. After a quick scan to confirm there was nobody else nearby, I whispered, "What about the thing that happened?"

Mimi whirled and pinned me with a flat stare. "Dead men don't get to be grooms. We're already working on a Plan B."

"You mean the wedding is still on?"

She let out an impatient hiss and glanced at her watch. "Yes. Why wouldn't it be?"

"Am I only planning a ceremony for one couple, then?"

She shoved open the warehouse door, glancing over her shoulder with an annoyed frown. "Don't be ridiculous. We don't have a show if we don't have two couples vying for the opportunity to have the wedding of their dreams."

"And half a million dollars," I muttered.

Mimi shrugged. "Doesn't hurt."

"You can't bring Beau back from the morgue." Images of a *Weekend at Bernie's*-style wedding where the dead groom was propped up like a puppet and moved between locations made my stomach flip. "Can you?"

I sucked in a deep breath and steeled myself for Mimi's response.

She stared at me for a moment, then amusement spread across her face. "Now you're thinking the way I need you to think."

I backed up a few steps. "Mimi, that's not—"

She chuckled, holding out her hand in front of her. "Relax. Legal said it was out of the question. And besides, there'd be too much press if we tried to leave the building for location shoots with a corpse."

I swallowed and bobbed my head. "People get a little put out when there's a dead guy on display."

"Exactly. Which is why we're shifting gears."

She motioned for me to follow her to the back of the warehouse, which was filled with large black prop bags and hard rolling containers. "Our new groom will be here this afternoon," she said. "And I'd like you to meet with him and Lily together so we can get fresh footage."

I kept nodding, wondering if I had landed in an alternate universe where a television crew was filming me for some sort of prank show. Unfortunately, either Mimi was a terrific actress, or this was all entirely too real. "Have any of the specs changed for the ceremony, given the new circumstances?"

"The only thing that has changed is the location. Instead of a beach wedding like we originally discussed, I'm going to need you to transform this space into a wedding wonderland." She swept her hand in front of her as if she were a talk show hostess presenting me with the ultimate jackpot.

Unfortunately, the prize in this case was a dark, dusty warehouse filled with cobwebs and rat droppings, and mere feet from where Beau Lyons took his last haunted breaths.

WHEN I ARRIVED home after lunch, I found Gage leaving Josie's apartment. "Did you finally ask her out?" I asked.

His shoulders slumped. "This wasn't a social call, I'm afraid."

I assessed Josie's closed door. "What happened? Is she okay?"

"You might want to ask her that. She could probably use a friend."

I shoved my way past Gage and knocked on Josie's door. When she didn't answer, I twisted the knob and nudged it open. "Josie?" I called. "Josie, it's me, Glory. Where are you?"

Still no response.

I passed her bedroom. The curtains were drawn, and the room was cloaked in darkness. I knew she had to be in there, so I rapped my knuckles on the open door a few times, then stepped in, flipping the light switch.

Her neatly made bed featured a bohemian-style embroidered coverlet in a sunny peacock blue with bright swirls of yellow and red stitching. I rounded the footboard and found Josie sitting cross-legged on the floor with her back to the mattress. With her eyes closed and her fingers resting upward on her knees, she seemed peaceful. Or like she was trying to levitate. I was never sure when it came to Josie.

I sat down on the edge, the mattress sinking under my weight. Josie still didn't open her eyes. "Hey," I said softly. "What's going on?"

"I'm hiding," she replied.

"I can see that, but I don't understand why. Did you and Gage have a fight?" If the solid hour of giggling afterward was any indication, she usually loved his visits. And although she had always denied it, it was clear their attraction was mutual.

She shook her head once. I had never seen Josie cry, but when she opened her eyes, a single tear slid down her cheek.

I hopped off the bed to retrieve the tissues from her dresser. I lifted it in the air a few times, trying to figure out what she had in there besides tissues, before extending it to her. "Are these things industrial strength? Because this box is heavy."

Josie yanked out the entire wad of tissues and dropped all

except one onto the floor in front of her. After she dabbed her eyes, she reached in and produced a hunting knife, its handle swirled with a delicate turquoise inlay.

She unsheathed the blade from its tan leather cover, holding it up to the light.

I took several steps back until my calves hit her night-stand, the lamp wobbling at the sudden impact. "Geez, Josie. Warn a girl before you pull a weapon on her."

"I almost forgot that was in there," she said with a loud sniff. "I'm not allowed to have a gun, but I tucked a few knives around when I moved in. It turns out you can hide them just about anywhere, then they're ready if you need to…"

"Stab someone?" I asked, eyeballing the exit.

She put the knife on the carpet. "When I first got here, I had never lived alone before. I kept thinking every noise was somebody trying to break in to strangle me in my sleep. I almost wet myself each time the garbage truck came."

"And you thought a knife would protect you?"

"Probably not. But I didn't want anyone catching me off-guard again," she said, her brief chuckle turning into deep sobs that wracked her shoulders.

I retrieved a handful of tissues and pushed them toward her.

"This is all because of those cookies," Josie said. "The walnut ones."

"You want me to get you one?" I asked. Sugar was Josie's weakness, so if anything could draw her out of this funk, cookies were at the top of the list.

I tried to stand up, but she put her hand over my fore-arm. "No. I don't think I can ever eat them again," she said, then started sobbing again.

"That's crazy talk. A life without cookies would be like living in a monastery."

"Or a prison," she whispered. "And I don't want to go to prison, Glory."

"They're just cookies, Jo. Nobody will arrest you for cookies," I said, then angled toward her. "Unless you did something weird to them. Did you do something weird to them?"

"No," she said, her breath jagged. "But it all started with the cookies."

"You're losing me here, Josie. What started with the cookies?"

She sniffled, then blew her nose. She crumpled the tissue onto the ground, then lifted another one from the pile, holding it up in front of her mouth. "The murder," she said in a muffled voice. "Beau's murder."

I squinted toward the door. "Gage doesn't think you had anything to do with it, does he? You were here."

She hiccupped. "Was I?" she asked, her voice low and raspy.

"It's not like you can go out anytime you—" I paused, thinking back to yesterday's visit to the health food store, when Josie had left the apartment for the first time in ages and wound up wandering onto a murder scene. "Oh," I said, drawing out the word on a long exhalation.

"I was there. I had the idea to go to the health food store for the walnuts so I could slip over and talk to him. I heard the noise. I didn't know what happened until later, but I was probably less than fifty feet from Beau when he was…" Her voice trailed off and she continued to take uneven breaths.

"Surely they don't think you had anything to do with it."

"But they do," she said with a whimper. "Gage stopped by to tell me I'm officially a suspect in Beau's murder."

After I made a box of macaroni and cheese from Josie's pantry and settled her on the sofa, I headed over to Beverlee's house.

I found her lying on her stomach in a patch of sunshine in the backyard, her bare feet stuck up in the air and a cellophane bag of trail mix spread out on the ground in front of her.

When she saw me nudge open the garden gate, she raised a hand. "Stop," she warned. "Don't move."

Alarmed, I froze mid-step, scanning her yard for the source of danger. "What is it?" I asked, hoping she wasn't about to point out a Copperhead poised to strike my ankle. Nothing ruined an already bad day faster than a venomous snake bite.

"Watch this." She crinkled the bag, then pushed herself into a sitting position.

I shook my head and let my foot touch the ground. "Beverlee, what are you—"

She pointed toward the far corner of the yard, where Matilda and her chicken pals were hanging out in the shady area near their coop.

Beverlee crinkled the bag again, and Matilda's beak popped up. "Come on, baby girl. You know you want it."

She made a loud snapping noise with her tongue, like the brisk tap of a finger on the stretched skin of a drum.

I closed the gate and crossed the yard, mindful of the grass in case Beverlee had forgotten she was saving me from being attacked by a rabid possum or an incoming flood. "Are you still trying to train your chicken?"

She sighed. "I even got the good stuff. A lady down at the feed store makes homemade trail mix for her grandkids, so I knew I could do the same for Matilda."

"You made trail mix for a chicken?"

"Sure. It's mostly mealworms, but I added some dried veggies for crunch and a handful of raisins to liven it up."

"I thought you hated raisins," I said, remembering how she had baked a double batch of oatmeal raisin scones for the ladies at the Methodist church when they hadn't invited her to their potluck poker night.

"For people," she scoffed. Rising, she brushed off the back of her red linen shorts. "They say, 'I despise you' in food form."

I checked out the bag and fought a ripple of nausea at the collection of crispy worms, oatmeal flakes, and dried fruit. "And for chickens?"

Beverlee tilted her head to the side. "For chickens, raisins are love. But I accidentally left the bag open last night, and they got a little stale, so I put it back in the oven this morning to freshen them up. Now they're just stale and warm."

I plucked a raisin from the bag and rolled it between my fingers, stealing a glance across the yard at Matilda, who was pecking at the ground and ignoring Beverlee's homemade treats. "And how's it going? Is she trained yet?"

She grunted and sprinkled a handful of granola on the grass. "I don't get it. There's a man on YouTube whose chickens jump through hoops when he blows a whistle. I'm only asking her to come when I call, not write a nuclear peace treaty. How hard can it be?"

"Have you ever thought about getting a dog?"

Beverlee refused my suggestion with a swish of her wrist, a wide stack of metal bracelets jangling on her arm. She motioned for me to follow her into the house. "Aside from insulting Matilda, what brings you by this afternoon?"

The fragrance of cinnamon and honey hit me as soon as I walked in the door, and I shot Matilda a glare through the glass. I sat down at the table and dropped my head into my hands.

Beverlee shuffled through the kitchen, slamming cabinet doors and rifling through the refrigerator. "Does this funk of yours have anything to do with that new job you refuse to talk about?"

"It's more about what happened at the job than the job itself. Although, that's a little weird, too."

She placed a frosted glass bowl overflowing with warm granola in front of me, then filled a mug with milk.

I looked around for the yellow ceramic planter where I used to dispose of Beverlee's culinary experiments when I was a kid. I wasn't above hiding chicken food in a Ficus if that meant I didn't have to eat it.

Beverlee gave a smug chuckle. "I got rid of that thing when you were ten. All those leftovers you tried to stuff in there started to smell like feet. Relax. It's worm-free."

I took a hesitant bite, failing to hide a moan of pleasure when the burst of cinnamon and sugar hit my tongue.

"So, are you worried about Josie's ex getting squashed like a bug by the light fixture?" She jabbed a spoon in the air. "Because you haven't lived your life right if that's the way it ends for you."

I couldn't argue. I didn't know much about Josie's ex-husband, but it took a special brand of jerk to let his wife take the fall for his criminal activity.

Beverlee plucked a piece of granola out of the bowl and popped it into her mouth. "Hollis said it was a crazy sight. There was no blood, just a giant glass chandelier that fell from the ceiling and then... lights out." She chuckled at her own joke.

"Did he tell you anything else?" I leaned forward onto my elbows and earned a hard stare from Beverlee. "Anything about, say, who was responsible? Or what made him think it wasn't an accident?"

"Just that he was out there most of the night trying to put all the pieces together. He said it seemed like somebody had gone after the rope that held up the chandelier because light fixtures don't crash to the ground on their own."

I sucked in a breath and flashed to a picture of Josie's apartment, which overflowed with incense, crystals, art supplies, and a very capable knife.

But Josie wasn't the slice-and-dice type. If she were going to kill somebody, she wouldn't stage an engineering accident. She'd just knock them over the head with one of her over-sized Himalayan salt lamps.

"Why all these questions?"

I wasn't sure how much information to share with her. But Beverlee was better at getting secrets out of people than the CIA, so I figured she already knew more than me, anyway.

"It's Josie," I said. "She's in trouble."

Beverlee's bright red lips paused midway through a sip of the tea she had been drinking out of a mason jar. "Because she might have killed her husband?"

I nodded.

She slowly lowered the glass and drummed her fingers on the table. "Seems to me like he might have deserved it."

"She didn't kill him," I replied. "At least I don't think she did."

"Of course not," Beverlee agreed. "Hollis said they requested the GPS records from her ankle monitor. Hopefully, once those come in, she'll be off the hook. They should prove she wasn't there."

"Are you supposed to know all of this?" I asked.

Beverlee shifted her cleavage and winked. "Probably not."

6

I arrived on the set that afternoon to find Jason and Hazel filming in a corner of the studio that had been transformed to resemble an upscale bistro. Because the show's contract specified the couples couldn't appear together in public before the official airing date, the designers had worked overtime to create the intimate scene.

The two contestants sat on the same side of a mahogany booth lined with black leather upholstery. A watercolor painting of parrots hung on a faux wood-paneled wall behind them, and long strands of ivy trailed from a basket hung in the corner to disguise the microphones capturing their conversation.

They were leaning toward each other, Hazel's hand resting on Jason's arm, his well-defined biceps on display even through the charcoal fabric of his blazer. She watched him with intensity, occasionally throwing her head back in an exaggerated laugh.

An actor with brown hair curling out from underneath a burgundy beret stood off to the side of the set with a bottle of champagne. Mimi acknowledged him as I shuffled past.

"Make sure the label is out when you're pouring," she said, turning to me with a dramatic eye roll. "Sponsors," she explained.

She snapped her fingers in front of my face and motioned for me to follow her. Since the entire staff was watching, I decided against tripping her on our way out. But it was a close call.

I trailed behind her until we reached the back corner of the warehouse, where several rolling carts of clothes formed a makeshift wall around a row of pleather styling chairs. In the center, a wooden stool sat in front of a full-length mirror surrounded by lights on tall metal poles. I swallowed. Either I was getting ready to face the inquisition or perform a striptease.

I jumped when Mimi's hand clamped over my shoulder to push me toward a seat. "Rocco will do your hair and makeup for the shoot today."

"Rocco?"

"He's a genius. You're in excellent hands," Mimi gushed, then bent close to my ear. "A little advice, though. Don't get him started on politics or whether women should have extensions after forty." Her fingers mimed scissors that took a sinister turn as she circled them around her temples.

Great. Not only did I have to figure out who murdered Beau Lyons, but I'd have to do it while an age-phobic Edward Scissorhands applied my eyeliner.

I started to ask if I could call my own hairstylist for the shoot. Even though she gossiped like it was her job, at least she wasn't crazy. But Mimi had abandoned me, her heels clicking on the concrete floor as she walked away.

For a moment, I stood there and pondered what to do. I was just about to make my escape when voices drifted from the far side of the warehouse.

"Did you see all the press out there this morning?" a

female asked. "I haven't seen that many photographers since I took my top off in *Playboy*. Who knew all it would take was a dead body?"

"The tabloids are having a field day with Beau's death," a man replied. "Be careful or you'll end up on the homepage of *The Enchanted Tattler* like Lily."

When they turned the corner into the makeup area, they halted and gaped at me with wide eyes, as if someone had pressed the pause button on their conversation, until I raised a hand in greeting.

"You must be Hazel," I said as I took her in.

She was abnormally tall and had spindly thighs that conjured up memories of the granddaddy longlegs I used to play with when I was a child. Her glossy black hair was tossed up in a messy bun that appeared haphazard, but I'm sure had taken her a while to get perfect. Large diamond studs sparkled beneath the artfully arranged tendrils. She had pale, creamy skin, high cheekbones, and shiny red lips that looked like she had been stung by a yellowjacket.

Hazel didn't respond. Instead, she crossed the room and sank onto the stool with a petulant whine. Too bad it wasn't a fainting couch, because it was apparent this woman was used to causing a scene. I made a mental note of her behavior because dramatic clients required special handling.

Her companion stepped forward with a friendly grin and an outstretched hand. "Yes, that frosty wench is Hazel. I'm Rocco Sabatino." He easily stood a few inches over six feet tall, and his wild mass of black hair looked like it had been ejected violently from his scalp. He walked around me in a slow circle, inspecting me from every angle. "And you are?"

"I'm the wedding planner," I said, wiggling my fingers at Hazel. "I'm the one who is going to make your big day glamorous."

That was all Hazel needed to hear. She sat up straighter

ERIN SCOGGINS

on the stool and gave me a chilly smile. She offered her hand, palm down, and I wondered if she wanted me to kiss it like she was the Pope. I hoped not. I would do a lot for this job, but I drew the line at putting my mouth on a potential killer, even if she had skin like Snow White.

Eventually, she tugged her hand back into her lap with a pout. "Mimi told us she had hired the best wedding planners in the area," she said, her tone crisp.

"Planner," I corrected. "It's just me."

From behind me, someone cleared their throat. I turned to see Mimi standing with Magnolia Winters, my lifelong nemesis, and the only other wedding planner to call Flat Falls home.

"I realized I was asking an awful lot of you to get so much done in such a limited amount of time," Mimi said. "So I reached out to the team at Weddings by the Sea, and Magnolia here was kind enough to agree to jump in and help."

Maggie beamed next to her in a pale blue sundress with thin spaghetti straps and yellow wedge sandals, a sleek cream-colored leather briefcase clutched between her manicured fingers. She gave a breezy wave.

I took a deep, grounding breath so I didn't inadvertently leap across the room to knock her down. "Maggie, how lovely to see you," I said from between gritted teeth. "I was so glad to hear that your time in prison didn't cause you too much grief."

She had spent a few days behind bars when she got wrapped up in the last murder in Flat Falls. Unfortunately, they didn't keep her.

Maggie shifted back on her heels and acknowledged me with a stiff nod and pursed lips. "Thank you for your concern, Glory. It was a trying time, for sure. But a Southern belle bounces right back after a challenge. It's in our genes."

Mimi seemed delighted that we knew each other and oblivious to the undercurrent of tension that stretched the length of the room. "Oh, good. I don't need to make introductions."

Flat Falls was a small town whose residents wielded an above-average capacity for holding grudges. Maggie Winters had been a dark cloud over my life since I was a child, when she stuck my hands in warm water at a slumber party. After I peed in my sleeping bag, she called me Potty Pants for the next decade. It was hard to let that kind of humiliation go.

"We've known each other for ages." I glared at Maggie before turning to Mimi. "But you didn't mention you might hire a second wedding planner for this project."

Mimi glanced up from her clipboard. "We weren't planning to hire anyone else. But then again, we weren't planning on this turning into quite the media spectacle it has become, either. We figured with all the extra publicity we're going to be getting, we might want to up the ante a bit. So we talked to the guys in the suits to increase the budget and... surprise!"

She opened her arms wide and grinned, entirely too cheerful for a woman who had just hand-delivered a demon and ruined my chance to pull this wedding off on my own.

⁓

THE DAY PASSED QUICKLY as we measured the warehouse space and documented the locations of power outlets and potential water supplies for the flock of doves Hazel insisted she wanted us to release just before the officiant declared the winning couple and ushered them down the aisle.

I rolled my shoulders and glanced at Maggie, who was staring into the corner chewing on the end of a pen.

"It's not too late to back out," I said.

67

She smirked. "Glory, backing out is not my style. You'll just have to deal with it."

I crossed my arms. "If we're going to do this, we need to figure out a way to divide and conquer. Mimi was right. This job is too big for one person."

"Did she say that?" Maggie pursed her lips, then raked a gaze down the front of my body. "Or did she say one person was too big for the job?"

Sucking in my stomach to hide my fondness for cherry milkshakes and loaded French fries, I dropped my clenched fists to my sides. Where Maggie was all long legs and swan-like neck, I was shorter and rounder, and she had accepted every opportunity to remind me of that fact since we were kids.

I had just taken an aggressive step toward her when I heard several voices approaching. Instead of letting my new client find me sprawled on top of the other wedding planner in a World Wrestling Federation-style battle for ultimate domination, I quickly flipped open my notes, intently studying the only inspiration I had been able to muster that morning: a four-inch square box with the word *warehouse* hastily scribbled across it.

I feigned surprise when Mimi led a handsome man with shiny dark hair, glasses, and three-day-old beard scruff into the room. He resembled a high-school physics teacher—if your high school was in Beverly Hills or filled with superheroes.

Then he flashed straight white teeth and a chin dimple like he was brandishing a weapon. Clark Kent had nothing on this guy.

"Oh, good," Mimi said. "You're both still here." She gestured toward the man. "Our savior has arrived."

I raised a brow and greeted him with a handshake. "That's a big title. I'm Glory Wells, the wedding planner."

"I'm not sure about the savior part, but I am here to help." Unlike Hazel, he shook my hand, his palm warm and soft. "Dan Nichols."

He looked familiar, but I couldn't place his name. Maggie distracted me when she straightened herself to her nearly six-foot height and ambled forward with a breathy sigh.

"Magnolia Winters." She brushed her fingers against his forearm for a moment, then shot me a pointed glare. "The other wedding planner."

"It appears I'll be in expert hands," he replied. "Tell me, is it odd for a groom to see the wedding planners before he gets a glimpse of the actual bride?"

Suddenly, a wave of understanding hit me. Dan Nichols was the new groom. The one who was replacing a corpse.

"You're doing fine," Mimi said, scanning the room. "Where is Rocco? We need Dan in hair and wardrobe before the big reveal."

Dan dipped his chin to stare at his black polo shirt and starched jeans. "Wardrobe?" he asked.

Mimi gave his arm a caress disguised as a squeeze before finally letting go. "No worries," she said. "It's nothing a good sport coat can't fix."

I covered my snort with a cough, then pretended to study my notes. When I looked up again, Dan was still watching me. Before he followed Mimi from the room, he gave me a quick wink.

"Don't even think about it." Maggie appraised me, her lips puckered. "You're not ruining this for us by going all floozy on the new groom. We all know about your poor decisions when it comes to men."

It was no secret I left Flat Falls the first time to run off and marry a man who turned out to be a thief, but his crimes weren't my fault.

My fault was loving him to begin with.

But I wouldn't offer Maggie the satisfaction of seeing my regret. Instead, I donned my sweetest smile. "Let's not focus on marriages of the past. Why don't we head over and see if we can catch the first meeting between Dan and Lily? I do love a good happily ever after, don't you?"

WHILE DAN WAS IN WARDROBE, I walked over to the living room set and found Lily seated on an upholstered chair, hands crossed primly in her lap.

Mimi was hovering nearby with her ever-present clipboard. "We're going to do a voiceover with a quick montage of you and Beau, finishing with the scenes we shot this morning at the cemetery."

I leaned in to whisper to a production assistant standing near the edge of the set. "They've already had Beau's funeral?"

She chuckled. "Mimi didn't want to wait for the actual service, so she had them create a fake one so they could film it."

"And how did that go?"

"She didn't think Lily looked heartbroken enough, so she brought in somebody to mist her face so her mascara smeared."

When the director signaled the crew to start filming again, silence fell over the crowd like a soggy afghan. Everyone stared at their feet until the lighting shifted, and the show's host sat down on the sofa next to Lily.

Javier's chestnut hair was pulled back in a man bun, but the rest of him looked like a burnt yeast roll from Beverlee's Thanksgiving table. He was dressed in a rust-colored shirt with ruffles flaring along his wrists. Dark skinny jeans compressed his lower body, and the overflow rose beyond his waistline and strained the buttons all the way up to a white fur bolero jacket that looked an awful lot like mashed potatoes.

"You came here to discover love," he said, offering Lily a tissue. "And so far, all you've found is heartbreak."

She sniffed and patted the tissue to her nose.

Javier spoke to the camera. "Well, folks, something unusual has happened. Something that has never occurred here at *Romance Revival.* We lost one groom, but another has gallantly come forward to take his place."

He paused, no doubt leaving space for the editors to insert gasps and applause from an invisible audience.

Before I could gag from my disgust, a flash of movement from the side of the stage caught my attention. Dan Nichols had moved to the edge of the set, his eyes focused on Lily.

"We know you were falling for Beau, Lily, and we'd never want to belittle those feelings." After a dramatic pause, Javier continued. "But in the spirit of true love and happiness, we wanted to offer you this second chance at your second chance."

Lily nodded again, and the corners of her lips turned up slightly. "All right," she said hesitantly.

Javier raised an arm, and the fake waiter I saw earlier walked out on set and deposited another chair beside Lily's. "Sometimes the thing that takes us into the future is a person from our past. Lily, I'd like you to welcome Dan Nichols. We approached him after the tragedy, and he offered to step in and take Beau's place in the competition."

Lily didn't bother concealing her shock, and Dan sat down in the empty chair after awkwardly patting her on the shoulder during his grand entrance.

"For those of you just tuning in, Dan might look familiar. Not only is he heir to the Nichols Pickles fortune, he was also the other half of that romantic tryst with our very own Lily Page that set the Internet ablaze." Javier turned to the camera and fanned himself with a cue card. "The world knows these two have chemistry. But the question is: can they get past their feuding families to find their own happily ever after?"

I scanned the room to see if anyone else was as stunned by this twist as I was, but everyone sat quietly, enraptured by the engineered emotional turmoil they were dragging Lily through.

Javier sauntered toward the camera. "Can Dan and Lily rekindle their oh-so-fiery flame?" Javier sauntered toward the camera. "Join us next week to find out if true love can rise from the ashes of heartbreak."

The host stepped back and motioned to Mimi, who was bouncing up and down on the balls of her feet and practically salivating.

"Okay, people," she said with a clap. "Time is money. We have one more challenge to film, then let's get some B-roll of our new Romeo and Juliet reconnecting on the beach."

I didn't want to remind her that somebody died at the end of that one, too.

"Love is in the air," Mimi said with an overdramatic flourish as she crossed the stage. She came to a stop in front of me and flipped back a couple pieces of paper on her clipboard. "And we have a wedding to plan. Where do we stand on the set for the ceremony?"

I swallowed against the bile that had been building up in my throat all day. "We've got everything under control."

～

"THIS IS OUT OF CONTROL," I shrieked toward Maggie as we watched the crew set up a pit of green sludge underneath a rotating obstacle course. "Who does something like this?"

"You know I hate to agree with you," she said. "But this

really is next-level weird. Just this morning they were trying to get Jason and Hazel to make out on the sofa where the chandelier fell. The rope that held it was still dangling from the ceiling like a noose, and they didn't even clean off the bloodstains. They told Hazel to cover them with the fabric of her skirt. Don't any of these people care a man died here?"

A shudder rolled through my stomach. She was right. Beau Lyons was murdered a few dozen feet from where we stood, and aside from the remnants of police tape that were shoved out of the way for the film crew to resume their work that morning, it was like it never even happened.

"Do you think one of them did it?" Maggie whispered, skimming her gaze across the room, where the set designers were testing a propellor that spun slowly over a giant balance ball.

The film crew scurried around, while Mimi barked instructions. "It's possible," I replied. "But I don't know why anyone would ever kill another human being for a television show."

Just then, Mimi ushered the four remaining contestants onto the set. Lily walked ten feet in front of Dan, only pausing to glare over her shoulder when Mimi asked them to gather at the starting line.

"Okay, teams," Mimi said with a chipper clap. "Welcome to Honeymoon Falls, our version of an obstacle course. It shouldn't be too difficult. You just have to keep from falling in the pit and make it to the end before your opponents. The winning team gets an on-camera spa day and an extra grand. Questions?"

Lily raised her hand. "I'm sorry, but I don't think—"

"Exactly!" Mimi exclaimed. "That's the right attitude. You don't need to think. Just feel, trust your partner, and don't get a concussion. Head bruises are a nightmare to cover with stage makeup."

As the director lined the contestants up along a pair of narrow beams, I leaned in toward Maggie. "She seems awfully blasé about a dead guy on her set. Do you believe she could be behind Beau's murder?"

Maggie considered Mimi, then scrunched up her face. "They would shut down production if she were involved, and you've seen her schedule. There's not a single time slot where she'd allow such a disruption."

"Yes, but—"

"I think it's much more likely that your friend Josie saw her cheating ex on tv and took the opportunity for revenge," Maggie whispered. "I can't blame her. I have yet to meet a man who doesn't make me want to buy stock in rat poison manufacturers."

The last I'd heard, Maggie was dating an already-engaged political candidate. "What about—"

"Don't mention him." She speared me with a glare that told me she might not even need poison to kill someone.

A production assistant shushed us as the cameras rolled. Heavy drumbeats thumped in the background and a spotlight shined on a countdown clock at the pinnacle of the final tower, a monstrosity of ledges and scaffolding that made me dizzy when I looked up.

The contestants ran through the first few obstacles easily, dodging whirling rotors and barbells wrapped in colored foam. At one point, Jason and Hazel took the lead, scampering across a gyrating beam while holding hands.

When Lily and Dan got to that same challenge, though, she swatted his hand away and surged past him.

"Grab onto each other," Mimi shouted. "It will help your balance, and the viewers love seeing pecs in action."

Both couples reached the tower simultaneously, but Hazel brushed by Lily to start her ascent first. Dan wasn't far behind, his muscles bunching as he easily climbed each level.

When they were almost to the top, he reached out to Lily one last time. After a moment's hesitation, she slipped her palm into his.

He had just started to pull her up to the last platform when Hazel's hand snaked out and grabbed Lily by the ankle. With a wild screech, she gave a forceful tug, sending Lily plummeting to the airbag-lined pool of goo at the bottom.

Hazel aimed a condescending smirk at Lily, who was sputtering and squeezing green slime from her braids. "Take that, Princess," she snarled before scurrying up to join Jason on the platform.

Mimi applauded, and I turned to Maggie with wide eyes. "They're all crazy. Every single one of them is capable of murder."

7

When I unlocked the door to my apartment that evening, I found Beverlee and Scoots perched on my sofa, feet kicked up on the coffee table and a bag of microwave popcorn between them.

I studied their faces, then gestured toward the door. "I could have sworn I locked that this morning."

Scoots licked her fingers and held out the bag. "You forget. I own the building."

"Does that mean you can let yourself in here anytime you want to help yourself to my food?" I took a handful of popcorn, shoved it into my mouth, and plopped down on the chair.

Beverlee chastised me with the shake of her head. "One. This is not food, it's a snack. An appetizer, at best. Culinary foreplay, but not food. And two. You didn't answer my calls earlier. I came over here to make sure you weren't buried knee-deep under some ax murderer's back porch. Scoots saw me sitting on the steps and assured me we would both be more comfortable if we waited for you inside."

I groaned. "So, it's not breaking and entering, it's—"

"Hospitality. Exactly." Beverlee sauntered over to the kitchen. "Why don't I whip us up some dinner and you can explain where you've been all day."

I pushed up from the chair and followed her. "Unless you can make chili from ketchup and onion soup mix, I doubt you'll find anything to cook in there. I haven't gotten to the store in a while."

Beverlee's eyebrows wrinkled, and she examined me as if I were speaking a foreign language. To her, the idea of having bare pantry shelves was about as absurd as wearing white after Labor Day or going to get the mail without first touching up her lipstick. "Give me the ketchup," she said and held out her hand.

I dragged her back into the living room. "We're not making dinner from condiments. I'll call over to Trolls and order some takeout. Let me ask Josie if she wants anything to eat first."

Scoots shook her head. "She's not there."

"What do you mean?" I asked. "Where else would she be? It's not like she gets free rein over the neighborhood or anything."

"Before we let ourselves in here, we knocked on her door to see if she'd let us wait for you in her place." Scoots narrowed her eyes. "She usually has cookies over there."

I ignored her and trudged across the porch.

I rapped my knuckles on Josie's door. No answer.

I knocked again. "Josie," I called. "I'm getting food. Do you want anything?"

Still no response.

Alarm prickled along my spine. Josie was always home. By law.

The door was locked, so I reached under the magenta straw mat that said Namaste At Home. My fingers finally hit the cold metal of her key. I slid it into the lock, pounding on the wood again as I pushed it open.

A trickle of light filtered in through the closed curtains, but Josie's normally bright and sunny apartment was dark. Even the lotus flower table lamp was off, and she kept that thing on all the time because she said it helped keep her centered and warded off mice.

I paused in the doorway, causing Scoots and Beverlee to pile up behind me.

Beverlee's forehead creased as she examined the empty apartment. "Well, this is odd."

"Maybe she's napping," I whispered, then pointed toward Josie's closed bedroom door.

Scoots barreled past me and wrenched open the door to Josie's room. "Not here," she shouted.

We checked the bathroom, and I peeled back the shower curtain to make sure she wasn't lurking in there.

I rounded the corner to the kitchen and found Beverlee assessing the cabinet beneath the sink. "What are you doing?" I asked. "She's not hiding under the garbage disposal."

Beverlee straightened. "I seem to remember that under the sink was your favorite hiding place when you were a child."

She had a point. After I lost my parents, I used to sneak away and cry. Since Beverlee's closets were always stuffed with knick-knacks, I picked one of the kitchen cabinets to hide in, instead. I didn't think Beverlee had ever figured out my secret spot, though. "It's where you hid the Oreos."

She shrugged. "You would sit in there for hours. I didn't want you to get hungry."

I felt my stomach rumble and motioned toward the cabinet. "Does she—"

Beverlee shook her head. "No Oreos."

"But there's this," Scoots said from the living room. She held up a small black box with a plastic strap attached to it.

"Josie's ankle monitor?" I asked.

"It appears so."

Beverlee let out a slow puff of air. "Well, that can't be good."

"What if something happened to her? Should we call the police?"

"And what if she did it on purpose?" Scoots asked. "Maybe we should sit tight and wait for her to return. She'll be able to explain what's going on, and we don't want to bring the authorities in until we know she's in trouble."

Since Scoots was a lawyer before she opened the pawnshop, she was close to a legal wizard in my eyes. I settled myself on the edge of the sofa. "So we just wait?"

Beverlee returned to the living room and set down a plate of scones covered in plastic wrap. "Might as well have a snack to help pass the time," she said before plucking off a pastry and taking a big bite.

~

WE POLISHED off the scones and were working on a block of gouda from her fridge when Josie's door opened.

She burst through the door, laughing. Gage was right behind her, carrying bags of takeout food from the Chinese diner down the street.

Her eyes widened when she saw us.

"Guess we don't need to call the police," Scoots said with a pointed look at Gage's badge.

Josie stared at us in confusion. "Why would you call the police?" she asked, her forehead wrinkling. "And why are you here?"

"We were just leaving," I blurted.

"No, we weren't," Scoots said as she cut off another slice of cheese. "We were trying to figure out where you were." She cleared her throat and motioned toward the table with her eyes like she was enduring a painful muscle spasm.

"Are you okay?" Josie asked, her brows drawn together as she studied us.

Scoots stopped twitching and snuck a glance at Gage. "Aren't you supposed to be... you know." She picked up the ankle monitor and then dangled it from her fingertips.

Josie shrugged. "Oh, that. The old one was having some issues. We took it off and tried to replace it, but the new unit wasn't working right, either. Gage drove me down to the station to get me fixed up."

"By the look on your face, I'd say he did a pretty good job of that." Scoots chuckled over a mouthful of cheese.

Gage's tan skin had turned an endearing shade of pink, and he was studying his shoes.

An airy smile darted across Josie's lips before she grabbed the takeout bag from Gage's grip. "As much as I'd love to hear why you're camping out in my living room, it has been a long day, and I'm hungry."

She focused pointedly on the door. "So, if you'll excuse us, Gage and I are going to eat our dim sum in peace."

Scoots stood and sauntered toward the kitchen. "You have Chinese food? You didn't happen to get those dumplings I like so much, did you? The steamed ones with the pork filling?"

Josie gave Scoots a playful shove. "You've already eaten my cheese," she said, with a longing gaze across the room at the empty plate resting on the coffee table. "And apparently my white chocolate cranberry scones, too."

I nudged both Scoots and Beverlee toward the door and turned back to Josie, who offered me a sly thumbs-up.

Call me, I mouthed.

~

I MET Maggie at the hardware store the following morning to keep working on wedding planning. She got there before I did and was leaning against the front window, arms crossed, tapping the toe of her unscuffed cream pumps on the sidewalk.

I gave a finger wiggle. "Good morning."

She pulled out a notepad, along with a stack of eight by ten glossy photos she must have taken on her phone while we were walking through the space the day before. She fanned them out and balanced them on the paint counter between the wood stirring sticks and a pile of color samples. "Do we want to start with the stage or the pyrotechnics?"

Stifling a groan, I peered down at the list of wedding essentials Mimi had given us. "How about the swing?"

Mimi's grand vision for the pickle princess included playing up her farm girl roots by having her descend from the ceiling on a jeweled swing instead of gliding down the aisle like a traditional bride.

Maggie agreed with a curt nod as if this were a normal request in the matrimonial world. "Okay, we'll start there."

She shuffled the papers until she produced a sketch of a silhouetted bride on a wide wooden swing, the ropes decorated with light pink and white flowers, tulle, and glistening twinkle lights.

As much as I hated to admit it, her vision was better than anything I could have dreamed up.

"This isn't Cirque du Soleil, Maggie. I know Mimi wants to drop her from the ceiling like a trapeze artist, but we have to think through the logistics."

Maggie scowled. "I don't see why it wouldn't work. We can just add on to the existing scaffolding that holds the lights. It's easy to get to, and one of the crew members should be able to rig it up for us."

"The same scaffolding used to suspend the chandelier that landed on the head of her first groom?" I asked, shooting her a glare. "I'm sure that's going to go over well."

"We'd have it inspected beforehand, Glory," she said, clicking her tongue. "Obviously. And we'd bring in extra safety personnel for the ceremony to ensure her welfare."

I thought about it for a moment. It would offer the bride a dramatic entrance, one that would be memorable on film, which was the most important thing. I gave a resigned sigh. "You're right. And your drawing is nice."

Surprise flickered across her face. "That's it?"

"What?"

"You're going to agree with me? Just like that?"

I shrugged. "We've got bigger things to worry about," I said, then pointed down the plumbing aisle, where a man stood pointing his cell phone camera at us. He wore sunglasses and had the hood of his sweatshirt drawn tight over his forehead.

When Maggie wiggled her fingers at him, he whipped around to study a toilet plunger. "Just ignore him. Mimi warned us there would be paparazzi everywhere."

The hairs on the back of my neck prickled with unease, but I did my best to act normal. I glanced down at Mimi's list, and I lowered my voice to a whisper. "What about dessert? How are we going to keep a 'seven-tier wedding cake that stands no less than five feet tall' from melting into a gigantic pile of white slime in North Carolina humidity and under all those studio lights?"

"Oh, that's easy," Maggie said, gathering her photos into a stack and tossing her silky blond hair over her shoulder. "We'll just fake it."

I caught a gasp before it escaped. "A fake wedding cake?"

83

"Sure. Do you think all those Hollywood types eat real cake, anyway?" She gave a short bark of laughter. "Not likely. We'll keep a couple of sheet cakes in the back if they do. And besides, I know a guy."

"A fake cake guy?"

"Absolutely. He's a dream to work with. He uses cut-out Styrofoam for the base layers, then decorates with real fondant and sugar embellishments like ribbons and flowers." She fluttered her fingers. "And presto—a gorgeous cake that will last through a nuclear apocalypse."

I once read that the only things that could survive a nuclear bomb were cockroaches, which meant that during the end times, we'd be left with a gigantic phony cake and an army of frustrated cockroaches who couldn't even eat it.

Leave it to Maggie to turn faking it into an art form.

8

———

"What about roses or a long stem of white gladiolus?" I asked, flipping through a bridal magazine the next morning with Lily. "Something classic and simple."

She sat with her feet curled up under her in a fuchsia velvet chair in the break room, a half-eaten croissant discarded on the table beside her. She had been distracted since Dan's return, but this morning I was having a hard time keeping her focus at all.

I swiped my hand in front of her face. "Hello?"

She jerked back to attention. "Sorry. I was thinking about Dan. Did you know we met at the library, of all places? We both grabbed the same marketing book, and it was love at first sight. For me, anyway."

"I saw the video, Lily. I'd say he was pretty smitten, too." I found it hard to imagine anyone could fake that level of... enthusiasm.

"I almost didn't agree when he asked me to dinner. Neither of our families would have approved. Daddy kept telling me I needed to focus all of my attention on Page's Pickles since he wants to retire in a few years." She plucked off a piece of her croissant and chewed it slowly. Finally, she continued. "But I couldn't help myself. Even though my father hated his family, Dan and I had something special."

I shrugged. "I'm not seeing the trouble so far."

"After the video came out, his father gave him an ultimatum. Me or the company." She gave a bitter laugh. "He chose the money."

I craned my neck and peeked down the hall, where Dan sat in the hot seat, no doubt enduring an interrogation at the hands of Mimi's production assistants. "He obviously changed his mind, though."

When I swung back around, Lily's eyes were brimming with tears. "Maybe, but it's still all about the money."

"Then why did you agree when *Romance Revival* asked him to step in as the second groom? Surely you can find a way out of the contract."

"The truth is, I don't enjoy being alone. My mama died when I was eight," she said. "It was just my daddy raising my sister and me. He was a farmer, so he didn't know much about little girls. He taught me to hunt and fish, and I could climb a tree faster than any boy in town, but we were still about as girly as they come. The deer head on the wall in our living room wears a pink rhinestone headband to this day."

"I'm sorry," I said. "That must have been difficult."

"Yes and no," she replied, a half-smile flitting across her lips. "Nobody wants to grow up without their mama, but Daddy spoiled me rotten."

After the scandal, the tabloids had agreed. Their headlines called her a tainted heiress who enjoyed hanging out on the party circuit, but that didn't jibe with the woman sitting in front of me, tracing her fingers along a picture of a gauzy veil in a bridal magazine.

"I lost my parents when I was young, too," I whispered, a rush of sadness washing over me. "I know how hard it can be to plan a wedding without your mother there. But your father sounds nice."

"Darn right, he is," a loud voice boomed from behind me.

"Daddy!" Lily squealed and leaped up from her chair. She ran across the room and into the outstretched arms of a handsome older man in khaki pants and a Hawaiian shirt. His hair was more salt than pepper, and he appeared to be someone used to getting what he wanted.

"Baby girl, let me look at of you!" Odell Page bellowed as he pushed his youngest daughter out to arm's length. "I was tickled to get the call from these yahoos that you needed some help to plan your big day. We got here as soon as we could."

"We?" Lily asked, standing on her toes to peek over her father's shoulder.

"I'm here." A young woman with curly brown hair and a vibrant smile came running into the room. "Had to take a pit stop on the way in. He drove like a maniac for the whole two hours, and you know he wouldn't stop for a bathroom break even if the car was on fire."

She gave a small wave to the camera. "Hi, I'm Caroline. Lily's big sister. We would have gotten here earlier, but Daddy worked late last night. I was up past midnight, and he still hadn't made it home for dinner."

Caroline beamed at the camera before throwing herself into the group hug.

"I've missed you so much." Lily stepped back, still clinging to the pair. Her lower lip quivered. "Now it seems real. My family is here."

An invisible band tightened around my rib cage as I watched the Pages circle together, regaling the cameras with tales about growing up on a Southern farm.

"I remember the day I brought that miniature pony

home," Odell said, resting his hand on his jiggling belly. "You two spent the better part of an afternoon coloring his hair pink. Poor guy couldn't hold his head up in the barn for weeks out of the shame."

"That was all Lily," Caroline replied, lifting a finger toward her sister. "I wanted to paint him with those glitter paints Grandma Donna gave us for Christmas."

Odell looked directly at the camera. "If you have little girls, there can never be enough glitter. Everything has to sparkle. Resign yourself to that fact now, and it will save you a lot of trouble down the road."

"It's true." Lily's shoulders shook with laughter as she threw her arm around her sister. "Remember that time you insisted your prom date bedazzle his pickup truck to match your dress? That poor guy ended up with his photo emblazoned on the front of our high school yearbook in a lavender sequined cummerbund."

"That was only because you insisted it would look like the cover of *Cosmopolitan*." Caroline gave her sister a teasing smile before bumping her with a hip. "It didn't, by the way."

Odell wrapped an arm around Lily. "And get a gander at you now, all grown up and getting married to a city slicker who doesn't know the first thing about pickles."

Caroline's eyebrows flew up to meet her hairline. "I hope that's not true, Daddy, or else Lily's new man might have to come to you for some pointers."

He gave a gruff grunt like a dog that had been woken up too quickly, a quick burst of energy that settled into comfort as he gazed over his two grown daughters. "I'll teach your fellow about pickles if you want me to. Whatever you need, you can count on me."

Both girls burst into fits of giggles, while Odell blinked at them in confusion.

"So when can we meet him?" he asked. "Everybody's

been so hush-hush about it. I'd like to get to know the young man who's about to marry my daughter."

Lily shifted in her seat. "About that. There's something I need to tell you."

Before she could finish, Dan rounded the corner, trailed by a camera crew. He held his hand out to Lily's father. "My name is Daniel, sir. It's a pleasure to meet you in person."

Caroline crossed behind Dan and wiggled her brows, then leaned in with a stage whisper. "He's cuter than in the video."

"Video?" Odell asked, whipping toward his daughter with a wrinkled brow. "This is the Nichols boy?"

"Daddy, I can explain."

"Explain?" he asked, his loud voice echoing throughout the warehouse. "There's nothing to explain. This man took advantage of you and put it on the Internet for everybody and their Grandma Susie to see."

Lily's father was taller than Dan by four inches and outweighed him by an easy fifty pounds. "In the back of my truck, I have a chainsaw, a machete, and a deceptively sharp pair of pruning shears," he said with a scowl, his teeth barely concealed behind a thick, silver mustache. He withdrew a pocketknife from his pocket and flicked it open and closed. "Like I always tell my girls, a smart man comes prepared. You never know when you're going to need to cut something."

The two men stared at each other until Caroline finally broke the silence by swatting her father on the arm. "Daddy, stop it. You're scaring him."

Dan stepped forward, his palm held out in front of his chest. "Sir, if I could—"

"You most certainly cannot," he said, turning to Lily. "Go get your things. I'm taking you home."

Mimi emerged from behind one of the cameras, barely

concealing her glee. "I'm sorry, Mr. Page, but your daughter signed a contract. She can't leave."

"Then find her another husband," he boomed. "Because I will kill this man if he lays a finger on my girl."

~

WHEN I STEPPED out of the room, I had a lump in my throat. Sure, Odell was angry. But it was obvious how much he cared about Lily.

When Beverlee took me in as a child, I knew I was lucky to have someone who loved me so well. But now and then, like when I saw the camaraderie that wound through the Page family, I really missed my parents.

My mom was the kind of woman who let me skip the last day of kindergarten so we could test every ice cream parlor on the boardwalk, and my dad was just like Odell: surly, boisterous, and silly, with a heart perfectly shaped for his daughter.

Since I didn't have a tissue to wipe off the errant tear sliding down my cheek, I swiped a fistful of my cardigan across my face, taking a slow breath in.

When I glanced up, Rocco was leaning against the wall less than twenty feet from me. I stifled my gasp with my sweater before raising my hand to greet him.

"Didn't mean to startle you," he said quietly. "It's not often I'm able to get the jump on somebody."

I could understand why. Like Odell, Rocco was a large man, and with his dark eyes and crazy hair, he looked even more menacing.

A shiver skittered down my spine. There was still a killer on the loose, and it wasn't a good idea to be alone anywhere right now. I gathered my papers together and stood. "No, I'm glad you're here. I have too much to do to sit around thinking." I peered over his shoulder. "And besides, I think some-body is probably waiting for me."

"That's why I'm here. Mimi sent me to find you. She wants to shoot some footage of you and the other wedding planner and told me to give you a bit of attention first."

I tucked a loose strand of hair behind my ear. The late fall humidity had made it frizzy and combative, and even the strongest elastic band couldn't keep it in check. "I'm not sure there are enough tools in the world to take care of this, Mr. Sabatino."

He studied me, then scoffed. "Women like you don't get it, do you?"

"Get what?"

"I was telling Lily this morning that it's always the most beautiful ones who feel insecure about how they look." He beckoned me with his fingers. "Now, come on. Glamour doesn't wait for anybody."

I followed him down the hallway toward his makeshift beauty salon. When we finally turned the corner, I found Maggie already seated in his chair, a tangled twist of rollers in her hair and a creamy white mask painted on her face. She had earbuds in and was bobbing her head up and down and flipping through a magazine.

I ducked my chin. "Nope. Not going to happen."

He shrugged. "She wouldn't stop talking about herself, so I offered her the chance to test one of the face masks my Hollywood clients love. She only had to promise to sit back, relax, and keep her trap shut."

I lifted a brow. "I don't want a face mask, no matter how trendy it is."

"No worries," he said with a grin, then hunched forward and shielded his mouth from Maggie's view. "It's Crisco from the food service area. It was that or shrimp pate, and I was afraid she'd catch on if I made her smell like a seafood buffet."

I snickered. "So, smelling like fried chicken is okay?"

"Whatever works," he said, then gestured to the other empty chair. "Now it's your turn. I hear there's a lovely lima bean hummus that would tighten those pores right up."

My eyes popped open, and I backed toward the door.

Rocco laughed and pointed to the chair. "Just kidding. Sit."

I fixed my glare on him as I trudged across the room.

"What is it with all the ladies today?" he asked. "Everybody is so jumpy."

"Dead bodies do that to people," I replied.

"I suppose. But between you and me, that particular dead body wasn't an immense loss to the human population."

"You weren't a fan of Team Beau?"

"I just didn't trust him."

"Why not?" I asked.

"Despite looking like he just won the middle school science fair, he was too smooth. Said all the right things, gave her the attention she wanted, but I didn't buy it for a split second. Trust me. In this line of work, you get to see behavior that would make even your mop curl."

"Behavior like... murder?" My breath quickened, and I tilted my head toward him. "Tell me more."

"Oh, I couldn't," he responded, running a paddle brush through the back of my hair.

I raised a brow.

"Fine. Twist my arm." He took a wide-toothed comb and smoothed out my top layer. "Rumor has it he was trying to dip his bread in his competition's gravy."

I gasped. "Hazel?"

Rocco acknowledged my question by letting out a dramatic wheeze. "Although why he'd ever choose her over

Lily is beyond me. It's like choosing between prime rib and a truck stop veggie burger."

"Because every woman wants to be compared to meat," I said with a groan.

He ordered me to close my eyes, and then I heard the hiss of hair spray. "Don't worry," he assured me when he finished spraying, his breath warm on my ear. "You're at least a chuck steak. Maybe even a ribeye."

I opened my eyes quickly, ready to confront him for his disrespect. But he was wearing a wide grin, and before he turned to help Maggie wipe the Crisco off her face, he gave me a good-natured wink.

9

Later that evening, I was standing over the sink in Josie's apartment snapping a pile of pole beans Beverlee had received from a suitor at the newspaper when a sharp knock sounded at the door.

I wiped my hands dry on the back of my shirt and pulled the door open, surprised to find Gage motionless on the other side. My smile fell when I saw his ramrod posture and the crease of a frown between his brows.

Another man waited on the porch behind him, his hands clasped stiffly in front of his abdomen. Dark sunglasses covered his eyes.

I nodded a greeting to both men. "I'd say hello, but something tells me this isn't a social visit."

Gage looked down at the ground before clearing his throat. "I need to speak with her," he said, his tone gruff. "Official police business."

I put a hand on his arm, his starched uniform scratchy against my palm. "Don't do this."

"Glory, who is it?" Josie called from the kitchen.

I straightened my spine and jutted my chin forward. At

five foot six, I never had the luxury of being tall, but I couldn't let him walk past me without standing up for my friend.

False bravado raced up my spine until Gage's partner rested his hand on his weapon and raised a dark brow in challenge. Defeated, I stepped back.

Gage squared his shoulders and glanced toward the kitchen in what seemed to be a standoff between his job and his conscience.

"You know this won't end in a happily ever after for you and Josie if you do this, don't you?" I whispered, a tumble of sadness winding through my chest.

He didn't speak and instead gave a quick jerk of his head.

I moved out of the way and allowed him entry to Josie's apartment with the sweep of a hand. "It's for you," I called over my shoulder.

Gage took a deep breath, then stepped across the threshold just as Josie strolled into the room.

"Hey, Officer," she said with a laugh. "For a minute it sounded like something serious was going on. We're making dinner. Meatloaf. If you can stick around, you're welcome to join us."

"This isn't a social call, Jo," he said.

"Sounds scary." Josie swatted him with the dishtowel in her hand.

"Josie," I warned.

Her eyes darted back and forth between us as she finally caught on to the sense of tension in the room. "What's going on, Gage?"

"I need you to come down to the station with us," Gage said, motioning to the other man, who was still standing on the porch, feet spread apart and one hand resting on his belt.

Josie kicked out a leg, flinging up the hem of her purple peasant skirt and flashing him a healthy amount of thigh along with the ankle monitor. "Hilarious. As much as I'd enjoy a visit downtown with you, Lady Justice has grounded me like the bad girl I am. Unfortunately, I can't go on any dates without permission from my chaperone."

She was playing it flirty, but I could tell by her high-pitched voice and quivering hand as she smoothed her skirt back down Josie realized she was in serious trouble.

"We've already cleared this with your correctional officer." Gage pressed his thumb into his temple. "Please don't make this harder than it has to be."

Josie twisted her long hair into a knot she secured with a rubber band from around her wrist. She stole a quick glance toward the door at the other man before moving one step closer to Gage. "Is that why you've been spending so much time over here lately?" she asked quietly. "Because you're trying to get dirt on me?"

He ducked his head.

"What was it, then?" Josie's gaze frantically swung around the room, her voice getting louder. "Because it seems to me you were pretending to like me when all you wanted to do is turn me in."

Gage swallowed, his Adam's apple bobbing up and down.

I picked up Josie's sweater from the back of the armchair and tucked it around her shoulders. "Go with him, and I'll see what I can find out."

Gage stepped aside as Josie marched past him. "I was wrong about you," she muttered as she clipped him with her shoulder on the way by.

His gaze dropped to the ground before he squared his frame and followed Josie down the stairs. Just before his boot met the top stair, he turned and caught my stare. "Call Scoots and tell her to get the best attorney she can find. Josie's going to need it."

~

IT TOOK one phone call and approximately twelve minutes before both Beverlee and Scoots showed up at Josie's door.

"I've left Hollis an urgent message," Beverlee said as she brushed past me into the apartment. "Although I'm not sure why he wouldn't answer if he saw it was me."

"Maybe because he's in the middle of a murder investigation," I suggested.

Beverlee crossed to the kitchen, opening and closing drawers, her hands fumbling as paper clips and mail tumbled to the floor. She always fussed when she was nervous.

On the day of my wedding, we almost had to sedate her. Looking back, it was warranted, because watching your niece marry the loser of the century tends to get you agitated.

"We need to make a list," she said. "Why doesn't Josie have a notepad on the counter like a normal person?"

Her voice trembled. Nobody wanted to come out and say it, but Josie was in real trouble and we didn't know how to help her.

Scoots followed her, slamming the drawers and leveling an annoyed glare at her friend. "We don't need a list." She held up two fingers. "We only need two things. The first is to find out what's going on with our friend and get her back here to do her time in peace like a normal criminal."

"And the second?" I asked, almost afraid to hear the answer.

"We need to figure out who killed Beau Lyons."

I snorted. "Just like that? Isn't that what the police are for?"

"One would think," she said. "So Beverlee and I will head on down to the station and see if we can figure out what's going on in the wonderful world of law enforcement.

I'm sure Hollis would love it if you stopped by to check on him."

With that, she ambled over to Beverlee and unbuttoned the top button of her floral blouse and spread the lapels apart, so a generous amount of lightly wrinkled cleavage was now on full display.

Beverlee shimmied and dug into her purse for a lipstick. "What am I supposed to do while you're off coercing the sheriff to give up information?"

Scoots gave me an impatient stare and pointed toward the door that led across the porch to my apartment. "Your job is to find the killer. It's not that complicated, Glory. Just follow the evidence. Now get back over there and change into something less conspicuous."

I inspected my black slacks and bright pink short-sleeved sweater and pearls. It was hard to out-Southern Maggie while still acting professional, so my wardrobe choices these days were limited. "What's wrong with my outfit?"

"Nothing, if your goal is to sell wrapping paper at the PTA fundraiser." She tapped her wrist. "Time is wasting, girl. Get down there and figure out who had a motive to kill Josie's husband."

She grimaced. "Besides Josie, that is."

I DIDN'T CHANGE CLOTHES, but I did head back down to the warehouse because once the nosiness gene gets triggered, it's almost impossible to turn off. I also still had a lot of work to get ready for the wedding, and finding the killer was now at the top of my to-do list, just above locating a caterer with a funnel cake machine.

I brought my old Honda to a creaking stop in the

parking space closest to the entrance and sat for a moment to catch my breath before I went inside.

As I stepped out of the car, I caught a flash of movement out of the corner of my eye. Two shadowy figures huddled against the far side of the warehouse, their bodies pressed together, but I couldn't make out who they were in the darkness.

With shaking hands, I climbed back into my car, tugged the door closed, and exhaled a relieved whoosh of breath when it didn't let out its usual groan of protest. I squeezed my lids shut while I turned on the ignition. When I popped one of them open again, half expecting to see a chainsaw-wielding murderer right outside my window, I was surprised that the pair was too engrossed in their embrace to notice me at all.

Unfortunate, since in my nervousness I hit the gas instead of the brake, sending my beloved Honda hurtling across the parking lot toward the mystery couple with creaking ferocity.

My headlights flooded the side of the warehouse with a wash of light, catching Rocco Sabatino with his palms engulfing Lily's slim shoulders.

With wide eyes and an untamed thundering scream, Rocco dropped his hands to her waist, spinning her to his other side and shielding her with his body.

The Honda was as obstinate as Beverlee, so when I jammed on the brake, it took a moment to decide if it was worth the effort before stuttering to a stop less than a foot from the metal wall.

I put the car in park and opened the door, trying to appear nonchalant about almost killing them both. I raised my hand in a jaunty wave. "Hey, you two. What are you guys doing out here tonight?"

Like that wasn't obvious by the scarlet blush creeping up Lily's cheeks.

Rocco stepped toward me, his breath heavy. "What was that about, Glory? You're too old to have just gotten your driver's license."

I patted down my hair. "There's no need to be rude, Rocco. But... sorry for startling you."

"Rocco was giving me a pep talk," Lily said, swaying slightly. "These last few days have been... tough."

"I can only imagine," I said, trying not to frown at their obvious deception. "I'm sure it's very stressful, being on a television show, witnessing a murder, and planning a wedding all at the same time."

Rocco put his hand on my shoulder, steering me toward the warehouse entrance. "Lily's heading home for some beauty rest and to clear her head. But I'd hate for you ladies to be out here all alone when there's a killer on the loose, so please allow me to escort you into the building."

I turned back toward Lily. "But I wanted to talk to her about something."

"It's late," he responded and stepped between me and Lily, his colossal frame towering over me.

I tried to edge around him. "It will only take a—"

He pushed again, this time with more force. "No, really," he said, his voice grating with a menacing tone I had never heard from him. "I insist."

Rocco practically shoved me inside the warehouse, then disappeared outside to escort Lily to her car. When the door shut behind me with a sharp click, I recoiled.

"It's a shame the cameras weren't here to catch that top-notch parking job of yours," Mimi said from the other side of the room, letting the plastic window cover flutter down. I hadn't even seen her standing there.

I wrung my hands together and swayed side to side. When Mimi took a step toward me, I flinched again.

"Why are you so jumpy tonight?" she asked.

"I'm not," I said, rubbing my palms up and down my arms. "Rocco just reminded me there's still a killer out there."

I bit my lip and stared at the door for a moment before finally speaking. "Is there anything going on between Lily and Rocco?"

"That could be my next show." Mimi snorted. "The Princess and the Werewolf."

"I'm serious. They were huddled together in the dark doing... suspicious things."

"You're not thinking of Hazel?" she asked. "That girl gets around faster than one of those food delivery trains at the sushi restaurant. It wouldn't surprise me in the least to find her slithered up next to somebody other than Jason."

"No," I replied with a quick jerk of my head. "I think Lily and Rocco are having an affair."

Mimi lifted a shoulder. "Not here to judge—just here to make ratings. There's nothing the cameras love more than scandal. Except maybe murder."

10

W hile I waited in the alley outside the pawnshop for Beverlee and Scoots to return, impatience slipped into irritation as I checked my phone for the tenth time.

One thing that surprised me after my husband Cobb left was how bad I had become at waiting. I used to spend hours trailing him as he wandered through the farmer's market to find the perfect eggplant or sprig of rosemary, happy to be a peripheral part of his day.

These days, I didn't have the gift of time. Not anymore. I had to make this business a success, and every minute that ticked by without a killer behind bars reminded me I was a long way away from where I needed to be. I felt like a spotted trout that had been caught in a wave and propelled over the concrete seawall. It was going to take a lot of flopping to get myself back to the safety of the ocean.

I had just dialed her number when Beverlee's convertible skidded to a stop beside me like an out-of-control bottle of mustard. The top was down, and a power ballad blared from the speakers.

Scoots was either playing air guitar or having a seizure in

the passenger seat, and Beverlee's fingers tapped a rhythm against the steering wheel.

I stalked over to the car and leaned over my aunt to snap the radio off.

"Why'd you do that?" Scoots asked with a glare. "We were just getting to the good part."

I let out an irritated sigh. "It's Rod Stewart, there is no good part. You need more modern taste in music, ladies."

Scoots flung her door open and was around to the driver's side with her wrinkled finger in my face before I could blink. "Are you calling us old?"

Although she only stood to my collarbone, she was still formidable enough that I inched back and held out my hand. "You're not old, you're… classic. Besides, an old person wouldn't listen to her music loud enough to shake the paint off my apartment walls."

"Unless she's deaf, too," Beverlee supplied from the driver's seat with a pointed scowl aimed at her friend.

Scoots whipped around, and when she took a step toward Beverlee, I put my palm on her shoulder. "We need to focus. Did you get any information at the police station?"

Beverlee opened the car door and nudged Scoots out of her way. She stared up at Josie's window. "Things don't look good for our girl," she said. "She's in trouble."

Heaviness settled in my stomach as I leaned against the building. "What did Hollis say?"

"The warrant for her monitor's GPS records came back," Scoots said. "And they've got her at the warehouse near the time of Beau's murder."

"She was shopping for tofu," I said weakly.

She shook her head. "Yes, but that's not the only place she was. They pinged her within 25 feet of the warehouse door."

I thought about the Flat Falls waterfront. It wasn't large,

and the health food store was in the middle of the block of shops that ran perpendicular to the water. "They only know she was in the general area, though. They can't tell how close she was to the murder when it happened."

"Even if she were shopping for fairy-certified lentils or some other overpriced nonsense at the very tip of the store, she would have been about two hundred feet away from the entrance closest to where Beau died."

"How do you know?" I asked. "Maybe your math is wrong."

"I own the building, Glory," she snapped, her mouth formed into a grim line. "My math isn't wrong."

I slapped my hand against the porch railing, flinching when a splinter of wood impaled itself into my ring finger. "So she was nearby. They have nothing else."

"They've got motive," Scoots said. "And more than one witness over the last eighteen months who will testify that Josie was carrying around a Buick-sized grudge against her ex-husband. Not to mention the fact that she mauled him on national television."

Beverlee was leaning against the side of her car, hip thrust out, touching up her lipstick in the driver's side mirror. "Men are stubborn. We wouldn't be women if we hadn't wanted to kill one a time or two." She smacked her lips together, then turned back toward us with a smirk. "Or twenty."

Scoots agreed. "Yes, but if you threaten to kill one of them and he ends up dead, you propel yourself to the top of the suspect list."

"Surely Hollis knows Josie wouldn't do something like this, though."

"He does?" Scoots raised a brow. "She's under house arrest for embezzlement. The man responsible for putting her there just broke her heart by going on a reality show to find another wife."

I chewed my lip as I considered her points. "She didn't—"

She clucked her tongue. "Not to mention he was killed after filming romantic scenes with that same woman. By a chandelier. It's a classic crime of passion."

Beverlee nodded. "She's right. There's not much to argue with. Josie looks guilty."

"But she didn't do it," I said, tension rising into the back of my skull.

Beverlee fluttered her fingers in the air. "Of course she didn't. But Hollis doesn't know her like we do. He's going to follow the evidence."

"As he should," Scoots said. "The evidence doesn't lie."

"Unless it does," I said. "What are the chances that the GPS information was wrong? Or somebody tampered with it?"

"Slim to none," Scoots replied. "Despite what you see in the movies, the technology is pretty foolproof. If it didn't work, there would be criminals running around all over the place and the authorities would never know."

I pursed my lips.

"Criminals other than Josie, I mean."

Beverlee brushed past me and walked up the stairs. But instead of turning toward my apartment, she headed over to Josie's.

"Um, Beverlee," I said. "That's not   "

She reached under the mat and fetched the key. "I need to think. And in order to think, I need a snack. Josie's refrigerator has much more potential than yours."

I couldn't disagree with that, so I followed her through the door. "Where do we start?" I asked.

"Maybe with some chips and dip," Scoots interjected

from behind me.

"I meant where do we start with figuring out who killed Beau Lyons?"

Beverlee, who was already elbow-deep in Josie's crisper drawer, pulled out jars of mayonnaise and roasted red peppers and smacked them onto the counter. She continued to rummage around until she found what she was searching for. "Aha," she said, drawing an orange brick of cheese out of the refrigerator and holding it up in the air like a trophy. "Pimento cheese is brain food for the sophisticates among us."

We stared at her, slack-jawed, as she rooted through the pantry until she found the foil-wrapped remnants of the baguette she had brought over a few days before. Then she started slicing and grating, mixing ingredients and mumbling to herself in incoherent sentence fragments accentuated by wild gesticulations with the knife.

I glanced at Scoots with wide eyes.

She shrugged. "Everybody's genius works differently."

Once she sliced and toasted the bread under the broiler, Beverlee topped each piece with a dollop of pimento cheese and arranged it on an acrylic tray she found in Josie's cabinet.

She carried the tray out into the living room and placed it on the coffee table, then dropped back onto the sofa with a sigh. "Now I can think," she said.

I sat next to her, careful to give her plenty of room if she needed to think with her knife again.

"Right now, Josie is the only suspect for the murder," Beverlee said as she reached for a piece of bread. "So we need to search where they aren't looking."

She turned to me. "What did you find out tonight at the warehouse?"

"Not much. Just that Beau's wife-to-be is also getting cozy with the hair guy."

Scoots leaned forward. "Cozy like she was getting comforted by a dear friend during her time of despair? Or cozy like those pictures TMZ had of her doing the dirty in the food factory?"

"It seemed more like the second kind."

"Interesting," Scoots said with a smirk. "So her first man sold her out, another got murdered, and the last one likes to do her hair when he's not skulking outside the warehouse in the dark?"

"That girl seems to know her way around a pickle," Beverlee added with a bemused smile before taking another bite of bread.

I snickered. "She's a real big dill."

"But does that make her a killer?" Beverlee asked.

I shook my head. "I don't get that feeling. She seemed to genuinely like Beau. And there was no way for her to guarantee she'd be able to stay on the show. By killing him, she was risking the possibility that she'd be sent home."

"But if the hairstylist was in love with her, he might have killed Beau to get his competition out of the way," Scoots said.

I made a note on the pad of paper Beverlee had left on the table earlier that day. First suspect: Rocco Sabatino.

It would be a shame if he was the killer. That kind of hair shouldn't be wasted in prison.

"Speaking of competition," Scoots added. "What about the other two? Jason and Hazel. If they killed Beau, their road to half a million dollars would be a lot smoother."

I scribbled their names on the paper. "Let's check into them. The more people we can investigate, the more likely we are to find the killer."

"Who else would benefit from having Beau out of the way?" Scoots asked.

"There's the new groom, Dan Nichols," I said. "But he

didn't arrive until after the murder, so despite being an opportunistic scumbag, it probably wasn't him."

"He got here awfully fast for somebody that had to upend his entire life, though. Put him on the list."

Beverlee tapped her finger on the table, her silver nail polish glistening under the living room lights. "So where do we start?"

"We need to figure out who these people really are," I replied. "And to do that, we will have to catch them when they're not on camera."

"Most of them are staying at the Budget Inn near the bridge." I cringed, realizing I had broken my confidentiality agreement again. "But you didn't hear that from me."

"Well, let's go snoop around," Beverlee said. "We'll start in the obvious place, with Rocco the hairdresser."

"It's not that easy," I responded. "They've hired extra security to keep both the paparazzi and the Flat Falls nosy brigade away. They were hiding in the dumpsters, trying to get scoop on the show before it goes live."

"That shouldn't be a problem," Beverlee said. "We'll go over there together, and you can flash your employee badge to gain access. If that doesn't work, I'll flash something else."

I fought not to groan when Beverlee reached into her shirt and fluffed up her cleavage. "Isn't the point for us to be inconspicuous?"

Beverlee shuffled into her handbag and extracted a travel-sized aerosol can of hair spray, emptying it onto her bangs. "Glory, it's not possible for me to be inconspicuous."

Scoots thrashed her hand in front of her face to diminish the fumes. "When are you going to do this?"

I sighed. "They're filming a location shoot at the beach tomorrow. I'm supposed to be planning the ceremony, so I don't have to be there. Let's stop by the motel then."

Beverlee clapped twice. "Perfect. That will give me plenty

of time to get my catsuit ready."

∾

When I knocked on Beverlee's door the next morning, she was dressed from head to toe in black spandex. But to call it a catsuit was a bit too generous. Instead, it reminded me of a full-length Jazzercise leotard from the eighties. She was only missing neon green legwarmers and a Richard Simmons poster on her wall.

"That might be great for nighttime snooping, but don't you think it's a little bold for sneaking around today?" I asked.

"Will I be too distracting?" She ran her hand down the abundant curve of her hip.

I didn't want to hurt her feelings, so I bobbed my head up and down. "Yes, that's it exactly. You could attract too much attention when we're trying to fly under the radar."

At least that part was the truth.

"I can see your point. Be right back."

I released a deep breath and sat down at her table to await her to return.

A moment later, a harsh clunk near the sliding glass door made me bolt up from my chair.

Matilda, Beverlee's favorite pet chicken, stared at me from the other side of the glass.

I acknowledged her with a quick wave.

She continued to stare, then rammed the door again.

"Beverlee," I called out down the hall. "I think your chicken just head-butted the back door trying to get in here."

"Well, let her in," Beverlee responded with a sniff.

Matilda stood statue-still and watched me as I walked toward the door, but as soon as I flipped the latch and slid the glass aside, she sprang into action. With an excited squawk and a flurry of black feathers, she brushed past me into the kitchen and settled on a small footstool next to the counter.

"Check the cookie jar, too," Beverlee replied. "I made her some energy bites this morning."

With a grunt of displeasure, I tugged the lid off the chicken-shaped ceramic cookie jar and scooped out a sticky ball of seeds. I put one in my palm and offered it to Matilda.

She didn't take the treat, but I could swear she rolled her beady eyes.

I was about to tattle on her, because even Beverlee wouldn't tolerate poultry disrespect, but then my aunt strutted back into the kitchen. Instead of changing out of the catsuit, she had merely added accessories. A teal off-the-shoulder sweater stretched tightly across her chest. She had also wound a leopard-print fanny pack around her waist and changed her shoes from black kitten-heeled sandals to shiny gold sneakers.

A yelp escaped my throat, and I clamped a hand over my lips to keep a string of profanity from slipping out.

Beverlee didn't notice. Instead, she walked over and took the energy bite out of my hand and popped it into her mouth. She tossed a loving gaze toward Matilda. "It appears my girl isn't a fan of honey," she said, wiping crumbs from the front of her sweater.

"Did you just eat chicken food again?" I asked, nausea churning in my belly.

"She eats the same things we do, Glory," Beverlee admonished. "Nuts and seeds, fruits, vegetables."

"Her favorite food is sugar cookies, Beverlee."

Beverlee grinned. "Oh, that reminds me. I made her some fresh apple butter turnovers a few days ago as a part of her training. She loves them. Pull them out from the fridge and help yourself to one while I grab my purse."

Beverlee had always used food to show her love, but I wasn't sure how Matilda the Chicken warranted the good stuff.

I opened the refrigerator. Compared to mine, which contained a tray of fast food hot sauce packets and an expired gallon of milk, Beverlee's fridge was overflowing with colorful fruits, fresh vegetables, and enough foil-covered dishes to feed the entire high school football team three square meals a day for a week.

After I found the right dish and slid it onto the counter, Matilda trotted across the room and pecked my foot.

"Ow," I said. "Be nice or I'll let you starve."

Matilda made a clucking noise I interpreted as an apology, so I peeled back the layer of foil. I lifted a turnover off the plate and held it out to her. She charged it with enthusiasm, nibbling off a small bite and running toward the door. Once she reached the glass, she sized me up like a puppy, waiting to see how quickly I responded to her demands.

"Fine," I said, depositing the remaining pastry on the ground outside the door. Matilda left the house with a chipper swagger in her tiny steps.

The scent of sweet apples and cinnamon on my fingertips reminded me I hadn't properly fueled for a morning of breaking and entering.

I hesitated, but my growling stomach talked me into grabbing one of the chicken snacks. I moaned as the sticky syrup hit my taste buds.

I snatched a second one and shoved it into my mouth before returning the plate to the refrigerator. A flash of shame that I had stooped to eating chicken food tugged at my brain, but the intense sugar buzz quickly overpowered it.

When Beverlee returned with her purse and a knowing smirk, I was more than ready to hit the trail to find a murderer.

11

Even though it sat on a piece of prime real estate only two blocks from the water, the Budget Inn lived up to its name. Run-down and dirty, it had been too good for the roaches long before I had known why a motel would rent rooms by the hour.

Its large sign was crooked and broken, like someone had thrown a baseball through it years ago. A used pizza box stating No Vacancy in red block letters hung from a single piece of duct tape from the bottom.

The Budget Inn had always been a hotspot for both vagrants and partiers. I shook my head as I remembered tasting my first sip of Carolina moonshine in Room 147 during Zoey Tremaine's sweet sixteen party. Her parents had owned the place and apparently thought it was a good idea to let their only daughter have an unsupervised sleepover in one of the suites.

As I turned into the motel parking lot with Beverlee riding shotgun, we passed the Methodist Ladies' Book Club, who had gathered on the street next to the motel with cameras and autograph pads. They squealed when they saw my car, but when they recognized me, they backed off in disappointment. I gave them a finger wave, while Beverlee shot daggers at them through the glass, disappointed they were stalking not-really famous people without her.

A gaggle of photographers had assembled near the driveway. Two of them were playing cards on a rickety folding table on the sidewalk between them. A third lingered in the shade under the bushes, red hair poking out from beneath a familiar black hoodie. Yet another sat cross-legged with his laptop on the grass, long legs extended like he was on a beach vacation instead of lurking in a cheap motel parking lot for signs of second-rate television stars.

Beverlee craned her neck to get a better look out the front window. "I thought you said it was a secret that the cast and crew were staying here."

We came to a stop next to a man slumped in a folding metal chair, dark sunglasses covering his eyes. Unlike Jimbo, this security guard was squat and portly, the bald spot on his head almost reflective in the morning sun. I cranked the window down, and the guard hauled himself to his feet.

"I'm afraid there's no vacancy at the motel today, ladies." He said the words slowly as he planted his hands on the roof, making a quick perusal of the car like he was trying to figure out if we were a threat or if maybe we were carting around a buffet in the back. "And the parking lot has been reserved for a private party."

"You don't need to be so secretive, honey," Beverlee said from the passenger seat. I looked over and caught her giving the man a wink. "We know what's going on here. But my niece works for the show, so if you could let us through, we'll be out of your way."

"I'm not sure what show you're referring to, ma'am."

I leaned over to grab my purse, which was crammed next to Beverlee's legs on the floorboard.

He stiffened and reached into the back of his waistband. After struggling for a moment, he finally produced a Taser, which he casually rested on the window frame.

Nobody wanted to get blasted this early in the morning, so I held up my hand. "Relax, John Wayne. I'm just getting my badge."

After shuffling through the contents, I eventually found the ID, a laminated plastic card on a black lanyard. I dangled it out the window between my fingers.

He squinted at the card. His breath smelled like nicotine and spicy pork sausage, and bile rose in the back of my throat. "There's nobody here," he said. "They've all already left. They're filming off-site today."

I dropped the badge into my purse, finally able to suck in a gasp of fresh air. "That's okay. I'm just here to deliver some paperwork."

It took him a full minute before he shoved the Taser back in his pants, but he waved me through.

"Have a good day," I said, but I pressed on the gas a little too hard and the car lurched forward a few feet. The guard jumped back like I had run over his foot.

"Your coworkers are nice," Beverlee said, her eyes wide and hopeful.

I groaned. "We're not here for you to fix me up with a second-string security guard who smells like the inside of a diner bathroom. We're here to search through Rocco's room."

"How are we supposed to figure out his room number?" Scoots asked.

As we drove around the building to the registration office, I spotted a familiar rust-covered Chevelle. "I've got this. Some things never change."

~

I STROLLED past the swimming pool, blanketed with a thick layer of green slime, and nudged open the metal door to the office. If time had been unkind to the exterior of the Budget Inn, it had skipped the office completely.

Dark wood paneling lined the walls, faded where the sun had reached through the glass every day for decades, and heavy brown curtains hid the windows that faced the pool deck. A tiny black-and-white television, its rabbit ears replaced by fragments of rusting metal coat hanger, showcased an infomercial for miracle disinfectant. A housefly buzzed around my head, then landed on the worn Formica counter next to a vintage adding machine.

I ran my finger over the counter and left a trail in the dust. Clearly, the Budget Inn didn't buy their cleaning supplies from the TV.

When I hesitantly reached over and tapped the bell, a crisp, cheerful ring echoed through the empty room.

"Be right there," a voice called from down the dark hallway.

While I waited, I flipped through a tourist brochure for a fried seafood restaurant I'm fairly sure went out of business around the time Clinton left office.

A woman with frizzing hair the color of day-old mushrooms stepped into the room, her mouth full and half a glazed donut in her hand. "How can I help you?" she asked after she'd finished chewing.

"Hey, Zoey. Long time, no see."

She slipped on a pair of rhinestone glasses from a tarnished chain around her neck and squinted toward me. "Glory Wells, is that you?"

"In the flesh," I said, sweeping out my palms and giving her a quick curtsy.

She rounded the counter and wrapped me in a hug. As she passed, I got a whiff of lemon Pledge and powdered sugar. "I heard you came back to town with your tail between your legs," she said with a wave down my body. "But you seem good. All fresh and relaxed-looking."

"Um… thanks?" Shame fought its way up my cheeks, but I gave a quick shrug and swatted the fly away from my cheek. "Divorcing a jerk will do that to you."

"Don't I know it?" She let out a gravelly laugh that reminded me of her old Chevelle's grinding gears. "Been there, done that. Three times, if you want the truth."

With an abrupt zig-zag, Zoey reached behind her and withdrew a thick phone book, its edges yellowed and ripped, and smacked it on the counter next to me. "Got him," she said. "That darn fly has been buzzing around here for a week."

I tried not to gag as she scraped the book against the counter, the fly's corpse dropping to the floor at my feet.

"Let that be a lesson to all your insect friends," she said, brandishing the book in the air and pointing it toward the darkest corners of the room. "This is where bugs come to die."

When she was finally satisfied that she had gotten her message across, she turned to me with a grin. "I know you didn't venture all the way down here to watch me wage war on the Flat Falls bug population. So how can I help you?"

I took a deep breath. Zoey had seen me through more lies than most people, from skipping school to pocketing a pack of Big Red gum from the principal's desk. What if she figured out I was here to cause trouble?

"I need to leave something for Rocco Sabatino." I held out the leather portfolio I had grabbed from the back seat on my way in. Zoey didn't need to know that the only thing inside was my cable bill.

"Oh, sure. I can get it to him." Her hand clamped onto

the cover. "I wouldn't mind having an excuse to see him again. He's quite the stallion, isn't he?"

Sure, I guess if you like your hairy men to be potential murderers, he's not half bad.

As she tugged the portfolio, my fingers started to slip. "No," I said, snapping my wrist and yanking it out of her hand with one violent jerk.

Her eyes widened, and she took a step back.

I gestured toward the TV, now playing a morning talk show featuring the latest in male pattern baldness treatments. "You're sweet to offer, but I can tell you're busy, and the producer has sworn me to secrecy. If you can just remind me of his room number, I'll drop it by."

"I see I'm not the only lady who has noticed his charm," she said with a conspiratorial wink. She flipped through a box of index cards on the counter and plucked one out. "He's in 218, down at the far end of the parking lot on the back side."

"Great, thanks." Although I was glad his building sat away from the street so there wouldn't be too many nosy eyes on us, I was even more relieved she hadn't called the police because she could see through my plan to break into Rocco's room.

I gave a wave and spun toward the exit before she could change her mind. "It was good to see you, Zoey."

I had just shoved the door open when Zoey called my name. My stomach fell, a solid thunk that made my vision swirl.

But when I pivoted, instead of holding the phone, she was shaking a set of keys on a clunky brass ring shaped like a lion's head. "No point in you leaving sensitive information out there for anybody to get their hands on, especially with all those photographers prowling around. Want a key?"

I chuckled as blood flow returned to my whirling brain.

Although it often walked the line between just plain nosy and welcome-to-the-gynecologist invasive, sometimes I really loved Southern hospitality.

~

I PULLED AROUND to the back of the building and parked beneath the shade of a gnarled live oak tree, mentally willing my muffler to keep its cranky mouth shut, and warned Beverlee, "We're going to make this fast. In and out. We're just looking for anything suspicious."

Beverlee held out a small black case she had produced from the bottom of her purse. "I was hoping to practice my lock-picking skills while we're here. Scoots said she couldn't sell it because it had bloodstains on it, but with a baking soda and peroxide bath, I made it look brand new."

After a long, slow inhale, I jangled the keyring in front of her. "We have keys, remember?"

"I know, but maybe you could go on in and have a peek around while I practice," she said, bouncing in her seat like a toddler.

I pinched the bridge of my nose. "The point is to be quick, not advertise that we're breaking and entering."

Beverlee huffed, then got out of the car. "Fine," she conceded, slamming the door with a loud thud. So much for not making a scene.

The rooms at the Budget Inn opened toward an exterior corridor, a gloomy, grime-filled walkway lined with rusty windows and haphazard burgundy and gold squares that had been painted to cover shoddy repairs.

I looked over my shoulder, scanning for security cameras or an errant member of the paparazzi. Nothing ruined a good crime spree faster than getting caught on film.

I knocked on the door, but there was no response.

Satisfied that we were alone, I slid the master key into the lock and walked in, Beverlee close on my heels.

Rocco's room smelled like a confusing combination of mildew and bathroom cleaner. Two double beds flanked the far wall, with brown and orange floral polyester coverlets tucked crisply underneath stacks of flat pillows the color of day-old pancakes. Floor-to-ceiling lined curtains were pushed back, letting in light and showcasing a flurry of dust-speckled air.

Beverlee closed the door behind me and let out a cheery whistle. "They haven't changed this room in twenty years."

She pointed to an amber-domed box on one of the side tables beside a black alarm clock with flashing red numbers. "I wonder if the Magic Fingers bed still works. Do you have any quarters? You know, for old time's sake?"

I tried not to shudder. "I don't want to know. Let's just get this done and get out of here. I'm afraid the space-time vortex is going to suck me in and spit me back out in the wrong decade. And I'm not keen on being arrested by Starsky and Hutch when we walk out of here."

"I can think of worse ways to spend an afternoon." Beverlee grinned and stared off into the distance as if she were visiting a pleasant memory.

A low groan escaped my lips before I could stop it. I snapped my fingers and pointed at the stack of papers on the Formica table in the corner. "We need to focus. You can have your nostalgia time after we're finished."

She crossed the room and thumbed through the pages while I took a quick look through the drawers.

A moment later, I heard her sharp intake of breath. "You're going to want to see these," she whispered.

Her voice had lost its lightness, and my head jerked up at the sudden change in her tone.

Beverlee spread out a stack of pictures. They were taken

at different locations and at different times, but they were all focused on the same subject: Lily Page.

"These aren't publicity photos," I said, picking up a picture of Lily at the supermarket. It had been shot through a window, as if someone were watching her from afar.

Beverlee opened a folder and a collection of articles spilled out, printed from a prominent tabloid website, *The Enchanted Tattler*.

I scanned them, a lump forming in my throat. "These are about Lily, too. Rocco has all the dirty details about the pickle affair."

"Let me see," Beverlee said as she plucked the piece of paper from my fingers and started reading out loud. "'An anonymous source describes the family's deep shame and regret over the incident. Odell Page, the small-town socialite's father, reportedly put his fist through a wall at their corporate headquarters when he discovered his youngest daughter in a compromising position with the future CEO of his biggest competition.'"

"Sounds like Rocco might not be the only one with issues," I said.

Beverlee agreed. "But why does he have all these pictures here with him in Flat Falls?"

I examined the room. There wasn't a printer, or even a laptop. "Do you think he brought the photos with him?"

"This isn't a simple workplace crush, Glory," she said, her white-knuckled fingers gripping the edge of the table.

A shiver snaked down my spine as I looked around. Was I standing in the sanctuary of a killer?

Because Rocco wasn't just enamored with the bride-to-be. He was stalking her.

12

Later that afternoon, I was sitting on my sofa trying to come up with centerpiece options made from twigs, conch shells, and hot pink sequins that wouldn't make this wedding mirror a beach club stripper's retirement party, when my cell phone rang.

"Hello?" I answered slowly. I wasn't in the mood to talk about political candidates or be offered an extended warranty on my fifteen-year-old Honda.

"Glory, is that you?"

I didn't recognize the voice, but the background, noisy with the clanking of glasses and the upbeat beach music, told me my quiet evening of crafting was about to end.

"It is," I replied, apprehension roiling in my stomach. "Who is this?"

"It's Lily Page. I hope you don't mind me calling, but we're having a girls' night, and we thought you might like to join us."

I pulled the phone away from my face and stared at it in confusion. Even though I hadn't been a wedding planner for long, getting invited to party with a bride I barely knew didn't seem like a normal part of the job.

When I moved the phone back up to my ear, I shook my head and cleared my throat. "But... why?"

"Hang on a second," Lily said, followed by rustling and a low mumble.

"I've never known you to turn down an invitation." The voice, high and shrill, held a derisive Southern twang.

I squeezed my eyes closed and wished there was an Advil fairy. "What are you doing there, Maggie?"

"We're having a bachelorette party, Glory. What do you think we're doing?"

Although a decade had passed since we'd been in school together, her voice still had the same smug tone that said I didn't belong there. I could almost picture her look of impatient disdain.

"The location shoot ran long today, and Mimi mentioned needing footage of the brides having fun. So they decided to film an impromptu bachelorette party. Since I already had a meeting scheduled with Hazel, they invited me along."

"So why did you call me?" I asked. The notion that Maggie and I were suddenly buddies didn't sit well with me, and the entire conversation had me feeling like I was walking through a funhouse waiting for someone in a creepy clown costume to jump out and scare me.

"It was Mimi's idea."

There we go.

"Fine," I said, studying the sweatpants and tank top I had thrown on earlier. "Give me half an hour."

I WRIGGLED into my only little black dress and twisted my hair up into a bun. I added a swipe of blush and mascara and finished with a bright red lipstick that had fallen out of Beverlee's purse and into my sofa cushions.

After arriving with seven minutes to spare, I did a final armpit sniff and yanked open the door to Trolls.

The restaurant was more crowded than normal, and it took me a moment to find the group of giggling women crammed together next to the bar. I wound my way around the camera crew and headed toward them.

With her elbow on the bar and her sister Caroline seated beside her, Lily appeared to be holding court. The other women, including Hazel and Maggie, fanned out in a semi-circle. Beyond them, a crowd of onlookers mingled with the *Romance Revival* team, giddy to be on the outskirts of celebrity.

Lily was the first to see me. She hopped off her barstool and ran over to greet me with a chipper hug. "You came."

I caught a glimpse of the camera, its red light flashing less than a few feet away.

Nobody wanted a grumpy wedding planner who would rather spend the evening at home in her pajamas, so I manu-factured a smile. "Wouldn't have missed it."

She tugged me toward the bar. "Come have a drink. Do you like sangria?"

I eyed the pitcher of dark wine filled with cinnamon sticks and bright slices of oranges, lemons, and green apples. Sangria was one of my favorites, but only because it always made me think of the person who could make it better than anyone else.

"Do you know Ian?" Lily asked as I finally noticed him leaning against the wall at the other end of the bar. His mouth curved up into a slow smile, and the room suddenly felt about ten degrees warmer and a hundred square feet smaller.

I heard a chuckle from behind me and I turned to see

Maggie, who was pulling a glass of chardonnay away from her lips. "Yes, you could say they know each other."

Lily looked back and forth between me and Ian and bounced on her stool. "I had forgotten what a small town this is, and this seems like an interesting conversation. Tell us everything."

I shrugged and reached for a glass from the bar. "Nothing to tell. Really."

"Don't be so modest, Glory," Maggie said, then glanced at Lily. "Glory here was the love of Ian's life. And she blew it by marrying another man."

Caroline cast a doubtful glance at Ian, whose muscles were flexing as he wiped down the counter with a bar towel. "There was somebody better than him?"

Back in high school, Ian had been my entire world, the person who tethered me to the ground when I got a wild idea or found myself in another bout of trouble. But I let the promise of big city life lure me away from him, and it wasn't long before I was swept away by Cobb Mulvaney.

Cobb had sweet talk down to a science. Too bad he was a lousy husband and an all-around thief.

Sadness washed over me as I thought about the complicated history between me and Ian. But I wasn't about to give Maggie the satisfaction of witnessing me rehash my regret over leaving him behind, so I took a hefty swig of sangria and raised my glass toward the other women. "Tonight isn't about me. How about a toast to the brides-to-be instead?"

My eyes focused down the bar where Ian stood watching me, and I was only vaguely aware of the cheers and the clinking of glasses.

I lifted my glass again in a mock salute, then turned back to the group, hoping to hide the flush creeping up my cheeks by completely ignoring it.

"Tell me how the filming went today," I said to Lily. "How is Dan?"

Lily's smile wavered. "He was fine. Mimi said the camera loves him."

Caroline gave her sister's arm a gentle squeeze. "He seems like a nice guy. Kind of quiet, but maybe a pleasant, stable businessman is just what you need right now."

"I don't think Daddy's ever going to bury that hatchet, though," Lily said. "I overheard him on the phone this morning with his lawyer, trying to figure out if there's a lawsuit hidden around here somewhere."

"Are you kidding?" she scoffed. "Everybody knows you have questionable taste in men, and he forgave you for bringing that wrestler home, even though that guy broke Dad's favorite chair during his after-dinner show."

"Mmmm," Lily murmured, her attention riveted on something else.

I followed her stare.

Rocco sat, unmoving, in a dark corner across the room. Watching, like a predator.

"Is he bothering you?" I asked, anxiety prickling my skin.

Her gaze held Rocco's for a few moments before she turned back to the group, finishing the rest of her drink in one long swallow. She set her glass down on the bar. "He's not bothering me at all," she said with a soft shake of her head as an upbeat song played through the speakers. "And I'm ready to dance."

"You heard the bride," I said, pointing toward the center of the room where all the tables had been shoved to the side to form a dance floor. "It's time to cut a rug."

A small, pulsing crowd gathered behind them, and the sangria-fueled group blended into the party on the dance floor within minutes, long arms and ombre hair extensions whirling through the air.

Lily's sister lost her inhibitions first, kicking her heels under a barstool before spinning back into the fold. Lily followed suit, dangling her silver sandals from her fingertips until she finally let them drop in a heap on the floor next to her. Hazel's normal scowl lessened into more of a displeased frown as she gyrated to the music.

The *Romance Revival* crew circled the group, with Mimi at the front of the pack issuing directions and making sure they didn't miss a single shot of the action.

Even the paparazzi seemed to enjoy the show. The redhead's hooded sweatshirt was gone, and in its place, he sported a casual T-shirt advertising a local brewery.

I hung back at the bar, hiding my chuckle behind my wine glass as Lily attempted an awkward version of the Running Man. She resembled the spindly needle on an old record player, lurching and weaving to the music.

"It's not nice to laugh at the less fortunate," Ian said from behind me. His voice was low and silky and, like always, sent a shot of fire coursing through my veins. "Not everybody had the experience of winning first place for her break-dancing routine to "Like a Virgin" in the school talent show."

Heat prickled my cheeks. "I was in the third grade, Ian."

"And I still remember you flashing your day-of-the-week underwear to the entire school while you tried to spin around on your head. You were wearing Tuesday." He leaned in closer. "But it was Friday. You were an untouchable rebel, even then."

I groaned, then pressed my forehead to the bar. "Don't remind me. Elementary school was hard."

I heard the twist of a cap and he placed a bottle of water next to my head. "Looks like watching other people dancing has gotten you overheated. I'm going out to the deck for my break. Care to join me?"

I stared at his outstretched palm as he stepped around the bar.

"Only if you promise to not talk about my underwear again."

His eyes got dark, and that elusive dimple flashed in his cheek. He grabbed the water bottle off the counter with one hand and hauled me off the stool with the other. "No deal," he said, dragging me through the crowd toward the back door. "That's one of my favorite subjects."

As soon as the door to the bar closed and I stepped out onto the deck, I took a deep breath. The weather had cooled down, a slight breeze stirred the air, and my brain wasn't being rattled by a frenzy of too-loud pop music and overly perfumed socialites. Bamboo tiki lamps flickered along the railings, their amber flames reflecting on the water that lapped up to the wooden dock. The whooshing echo of cars driving over the bridge above made the rest of the world seem far away.

Ian held out the bottle of water, and I accepted it with a nod of thanks. "When did I become the one who wanted to leave a party early so I could go home and eat microwave popcorn and watch a chick flick?" I mused.

I still liked to dance, but these days, I did it in the privacy of my living room.

Ian laughed and inclined his head toward the bar, where the muffled sounds of celebration drifted out. "What's really going on in there?"

I shrugged. "I'm not allowed to talk about it. Just trust me when I say you should be careful the next time you want to date somebody. People are crazy, and love can get you killed."

ERIN SCOGGINS

Ian raised a brow and leaned in close, his breath a whisper against my cheek. "I know firsthand how dangerous love can be, Glory."

A strange combination of panic and pleasure shot through me, and my eyes darted toward the door as I felt an impulse to run.

He chuckled and grabbed the water bottle from my hand, finishing it in one deep gulp. He tossed the bottle across the deck into a nearby trash can and grinned when it sailed in with a solid thunk. "Don't look so freaked out, Glory. It was a long time ago."

The panic slowly faded, and a thrum of disappointment took its place.

"Speaking of which, Hollis told me he located your ex-husband."

My fingers gripped the railing. "He did. He found an address up in Virginia. Cobb was working nights as a chef in a dinner theater that performed magic shows. Imagine that." My laugh came out more bitter and high-pitched than I intended it to.

"And?"

"And by the time my attorney got the papers up there, he had disappeared again." I rocked back on my heels. "He was fantastic at that."

"At what?" Ian asked, his voice kind and soft.

"At making things magical, then running away before anybody realized it was all an illusion."

Ian dragged his finger, still damp from the water bottle, along my jawline, leaving a trail of goosebumps in its wake.

"I don't expect to get back the money he stole," I said, shame rising in my chest.

"What do you expect?"

I swallowed, and a long second stretched out before I

trusted myself enough to respond. "The chance to confront him for breaking my heart."

I thought about the look on Josie's face when she saw Beau on the screen the first time. "That's what we all want, isn't it? The chance to find out why."

Ian leaned against a weathered wooden picnic table and studied me before finally responding. "I remember a time not too long ago when I had the same question."

His voice was gentle, and that gentleness was almost my undoing.

"I'm sorry I hurt you, Ian."

He stepped toward me slowly, and his head dipped as if he wanted to confess his sins. Or kiss me—I wasn't sure which was worse.

But just as he leaned down, the back door slammed open with a loud bang. "Ian, we have an emergency."

Ian blinked twice as if pulling himself out of a trance, then brushed past me.

"What is it?" I called out.

"It's one of the girls from the television show," the waiter replied. "She collapsed on the dance floor."

We rushed back into the bar, and Ian pushed his way through the mob. Caroline, her arms and legs splayed out at awkward angles from beneath the knee-length hem of her floral dress, was lying in the middle of the room.

On her knees next to her sister, Lily sobbed, her eyes frantically searching the crowd. "Somebody help her. Help her, please."

I squatted and put my hand on Lily's back as I tried to make sense of what was happening. Music still throbbed in the background, but everything else around us swirled in slow motion.

The bouncer ushered the camera crew out the side door

to the parking lot. "We've called 911," he said. "No more photos."

The click of shutters continued even as he slammed the door shut behind them.

Ian motioned for me to keep Lily out of the way as he crouched beside Caroline's prone body. He put his face next to hers, his cheek right above her mouth, and ran his hand along her neck. Ian paused for a moment to stare at the ceiling.

"She's breathing. Pulse is weak, but it's there." He focused on Lily. "How much did she have to drink?"

Lily shook her head, her eyes wild. "I don't know. Maybe... maybe a glass or two of sangria?"

The crowd thinned when the paramedics arrived and evaluated Caroline's vital signs with somber faces. Within minutes, she was loaded onto a stretcher and wheeled out the door, Lily right behind her.

Just before she walked out, she turned to Hazel. "I'm sorry, I have to go. Can you find a ride back to the motel?"

Rocco stepped out from the side of the crowd and pressed her sandals into Lily's hand, his eyes filled with worry. "I've got her," he whispered. "Take care of your sister."

13

I stayed and helped Ian clean up after the paramedics left, although most of the patrons wandered off not long after. Apparently, fried shrimp and frozen margaritas didn't sell well when people were confronted with their own mortality.

The camera crew followed Lily and Caroline to the hospital because nothing said good television better than an unconscious maid of honor being wheeled out of an ambulance with an IV drip, her weeping sister at her side.

Rocco and Hazel huddled in the corner, bottles of water in front of them, their faces still pinched and pale. Hazel's fingers moved quickly across her phone, while Rocco stared at the wall.

I slumped into a vacant chair next to them. "It's late, and I'm sure you've got an early call in the morning. There's nothing left to do here. Why don't you go back to the motel and get some rest?"

Rocco scrubbed his fingers across his jaw. "This is getting out of hand, and it needs to stop."

A bitter chuckle rooted in the back of my throat. "This isn't the first time a bachelorette party has gone off the rails.

I'm sure Caroline will be fine after a good night's sleep and some food."

"She ruined my party," Hazel said with a pout, dropping her phone on the table. She glanced up with red-rimmed eyes, dark streaks of mascara smeared across her cheeks. "Leave it to Lily to get all the attention. This will be all over the tabloids tomorrow."

Rocco let out a jagged sigh. "This project was doomed from the start."

I leaned forward, the table's metal cold on my elbows. "What do you mean?"

"You didn't hear this from me," he said, lowering his chin and casting a not-so-subtle glance around the room. "But *Romance Revival* didn't get the green light at first. Nobody believed a reality show about a bunch of has-been social rejects could bring in the ratings to make it worth the investment."

Hazel cringed. Not even a high-dollar concealer could repair her mottled face.

"No offense," Rocco said with an indifferent shrug.

I tapped my fingernail on the table, waiting for him to continue. A man like Rocco didn't let the opportunity to gossip pass him by.

As expected, within moments, he settled back into the chair with his lips pursed as if he had just downed a bag of sour candy. "I don't know the specifics, but Mimi comes from money. A lot of money." He paused, his eyes wide. "And when she couldn't get another backer, she begged Daddy. Word behind the scenes says he threw in the dough to cover production costs."

I shook my head, trying to put the pieces together, but coming up short. I needed Beverlee here to Southern comfort him into spilling his guts. She had the kind of face that made people talk.

After checking over his shoulder, Rocco lifted one finger into the air like he was testing the wind. "But there was a stipulation."

Bingo. I raised a brow and tried to hide my grin. Maybe my face wasn't hopeless, after all.

"Her father took a colossal risk on this project. So Mimi has to get the ratings or her big dreams of becoming a Hollywood producer are over. If she fails, she'll be blacklisted."

My eyes widened, and I fought to remain calm. Scandal was one guaranteed way to entice viewers to a television show.

The other? Murder.

IAN WALKED me home after Trolls closed, and the sight of Josie's dark apartment and the knowledge that a murderer was still out there kept me awake and fitful until almost dawn.

When my phone rang at eight o'clock the next morning, I ignored it. But after the third series of annoying chirps signaled I had a voicemail, I finally hefted myself up to peer at the screen.

I let out an impatient wheeze, both my brain and my vocal cords still wrapped in cobwebs from the night before. "Good morning, Beverlee. Can I call you back when normal people are awake? Say around noon?"

A loud thump hit my front door. "I'm outside, and I need to talk to you. Open up."

When pulling the covers up over my head didn't stop the knocking, I closed my eyes and groaned into the phone.

"I have coffee," she said in a sing-song voice.

One eye popped open.

"And a lemon blueberry muffin from the Grind and Go."

I still didn't move. Even Shirley's famous muffins weren't giving my enthusiasm a boost this morning.

"And a key."

"Fine," I said, the pulsing in my head starting to ease. "But you have five minutes, then I'm going back to bed like a civilized person who stayed up far too late last night."

"Deal," she agreed, disconnecting.

After throwing a ratty sweater over my pajamas, I looked out the peephole. Sure enough, Beverlee was standing on the other side waving a cardboard tray of drinks in one hand and a brown paper bag in the other.

I thumbed the lock and opened the door. Before I even acknowledged Beverlee, I grabbed the coffee and inhaled deeply.

"Good morning to you, too," she said as she dangled the bag in front of her chest. She craned her neck to peek over my shoulder. "Rough night?"

"Yes, but not for the reason you're hoping." Beverlee always wished I would fall in love and get married, or at least have a late-night tryst with a stranger. Truthfully, she did it enough for both of us.

"I heard what happened at Trolls."

I took a sip of coffee and pulled my head back with a hiss when I scalded my lip.

Beverlee shook her head. "Coffee is not a race, Glory. It's a meditative experience. One that should be savored. Like fine wine. Or love."

"No. Coffee is the trigger for my on switch. And if you want me to care why you're even here this early in the morning, you want me to have at least half a cup." I braved the coffee again, this time savoring the burn as the fiery liquid slid down my throat. "Speaking of which, you've already used up three minutes."

Beverlee elbowed past me and sat down in the living

room. She drew a pair of muffins out of the bag, smoothing it neatly on the table in front of her. She folded a pair of white paper napkins and tucked one into my fisted hand. "We need to work on your manners, dear."

I eyed the napkin. "Two minutes," I warned and plopped down next to her, my cup cradled between my hands.

She lowered her cup, and the corners of her mouth crinkled into a pout. "Fine. I just came from the Grind and Go, where I ran into Hollis. He was at the hospital all night, poor man."

"Caroline?"

"It was a little touchy in the beginning, but she's going to be okay."

I let out a deep breath. "Makes me want to never have sangria again, that's for sure."

"That's the funny thing, though," Beverlee said. "Hollis is planning to interview the witnesses today, but it sounds like Caroline didn't drink very much last night. She was supposed to be the party's designated driver."

Thinking back to last night's events, I remembered seeing Caroline with a glass of sangria in her hand, but aside from dancing and joking around with her sister, she hadn't seemed intoxicated at all. At least until we had come in and found her crumpled up like a ball of used tin foil on the floor.

"What happened?"

"Hollis believes somebody tampered with her drink."

"What? Like putting drugs in it?"

"They're looking into it. They ran some tests last night, and they've got a crew over at Trolls gathering evidence."

"Ian—"

"He knows. He came to the hospital to check on her last night."

I exhaled slowly. "He must have gone over there after he walked me home. How is he?"

"Worried. And not just because one of his customers might have been poisoned, but also because you seem to be in the thick of it."

I sputtered, sending a splash of piping hot coffee onto my wrist. "I'm sure he's more concerned about the press this is going to give his restaurant."

"Maybe, but he asked Hollis to help him look out for you, anyway."

"Nobody's coming after me, Beverlee," I said. "I'm just the wedding planner."

"Nevertheless, you need to keep your eyes open."

Beverlee tucked her napkin and the muffin wrapper back into the bakery bag and slowly folded it closed. "I have more news. Josie's due in court on Monday morning."

"But don't they see it couldn't have been her? Somebody else is behind this."

"Hollis thinks they're two separate incidents. Josie's revenge on her ex and the Hollywood-gone-wild drug culture, brought here by the *Romance Revival* cast."

"He's wrong," I said, the muffin lodging in my stomach with the weight of a boulder.

She patted me on the knee. "We both know that, Glory, but Hollis is bull-headed and focused on following the rules. He'll figure it out, eventually."

"But when? After Josie's in jail for real?"

I tore off a piece of napkin and balled it up between my fingers. "But none of this makes sense. First, somebody murdered Beau. And then somebody tried to kill Caroline. And so far, Josie is the only suspect. But she couldn't have slipped something into Caroline's drink. You can't do that from jail."

"Then we need to come up with enough evidence so Hollis can't argue with it anymore, and he lets Josie go."

"How are we going to get evid—" I stood up with a

jerk, a flash of dizziness colliding with the sudden realization that Beverlee was sporting her let's-commit-a-crime face. "Oh."

Beverlee gave a smug smile. "And there she is, ladies and gentlemen."

"As far as I can tell, the only thing those crimes had in common is Lily Page," I said, digging through the laundry basket that had taken up permanent residence next to the sofa to find something that could pass for work attire. "We need to get our hands on the footage from last night's bachelorette party."

～

"ABSOLUTELY NOT." Mimi crossed her arms in front of her on the desk when I stopped by her office later that day. "You can't have the footage."

"Why not?" I asked. "The police are going to come looking for it, anyway. We might as well see what's on it and get ahead of them if there's something on there you don't want be released to the press."

She hesitated, the pointed toe of her patent flat suddenly stopping its staccato beat.

"No." Her brows slashed toward the bridge of her nose as she shook her head. "I'm successful at my job because I can keep secrets. Reality television is all about secrets—how to uncover them and how to share them when the time is right."

"If there is any footage," she continued. "And I'm not confirming it either way... I assure you it has no bearing on the investigation."

"But—"

Mimi squinted toward me as if she were examining a stain on the rug. "Why are you so interested? You're here to do one job, and one job only. I need you to focus on the wedding."

I tamped down the desperation that was clawing its way up my spine. I needed this business. But I also needed to protect my friend. And unless I could figure out what happened to Caroline at the party, I wouldn't be able to do either.

I sank into the chair across from her. "You've never lived in a small town, have you?"

She wrinkled her nose. "Small towns make me… twitchy."

"And they should. They're filled with nosy people convinced they're entitled to know everything about you. If there's nothing to know, they'll make something up. If you ever do anything wrong, they won't let you forget it."

"That's why they make me uncomfortable," she admitted.

I held up a finger. "But they look out for you when you need it. And somebody we care about is sitting in jail for a murder she didn't commit."

Mimi waved me away. "I heard about that. I imagine it's hard enough to deal with being on house arrest. Then to be faced with the man you loved finding happiness on national television? Scandalous."

I studied Mimi's expression as she spoke, my heartbeat drumming in my chest with increasing intensity. But it wasn't just her flippant reply that made my pulse quicken. It was the flare of her pupils when I mentioned Josie. The memory of her smug grin as she had watched the ambulance lift Caroline onto the stretcher. The way she gravitated toward drama like she was steering toward a five-car pileup on the bridge to the mainland.

She wasn't a bystander to all the chaos; she was controlling it.

That's why she moved filming to the rinky-dink North

Carolina coast instead of staying in California. Why she picked Carolina Weddings over Maggie's better-known company.

She knew.

She knew Josie was here in Flat Falls and that we were friends.

She knew there would be a confrontation because she planned it from the beginning.

But did she know there was going to be a murder?

14

Hollis let me see Josie that afternoon, but when I elbowed the door to the visitation room and found her sitting in the corner, shoulders slumped, I had to turn away before she witnessed the alarm on my face.

Once I'd composed myself, I dropped into the chair next to her and pointed at the khaki jumpsuit hanging loosely over her body. "I almost missed you," I said, gesturing around the drab room. "You blend in."

With its biscuit-colored walls and eclectic collection of flat pine chairs and discolored laminate tables, the meeting area reminded me of a decades-old fifth-grade classroom. A bulletin board gathered dust in the center of the windowless wall, a ripped poster stapled to it listing rules for spending time with prisoners.

"I would have dressed up for you, but it clearly says we're not allowed to accessorize." I nodded toward the poster. "Do they think you'll escape out the window if I slip you a scarf?"

"It's worth a try," she replied, the corners of her mouth turning up in a half-hearted smile before falling again in defeat. "But you shouldn't have come."

Josie, who normally illuminated a room with a wide, toothy grin and wild gypsy clothes despite the scarlet letter of embezzler stitched across her chest, sat almost motionless with her legs tucked underneath her in the wooden chair.

Her hair hung in a limp mat that poorly concealed the dark circles ringing her eyes. It was like someone had walked over and switched off her light. There was no spark, no joy, and no smart aleck comebacks, just resignation that she was going to sit here in this cinderblock room under these depressing fluorescent lights and wither away.

I thought about putting on a false display of enthusiasm that this nightmare would end soon, but I couldn't lie to my friend. Swallowing against the sudden heaviness in my throat, I mustered up a grimace. "It seems like you're screwed."

She finally laughed, a low, rusty chuckle that didn't quite make it to her eyes. "Appears that way," she said, flinging her leg out and letting her heel hit the floor between us with a thud. "But at least I got my jewelry removed for a while. You wouldn't believe how that thing chafed."

I rested my hand on her arm. "We're working on it, Jo. Have they set a bail amount for you yet? I don't have much, but I'm sure we can scrape together enough to—"

"It's a million dollars."

I cleared my throat. "Huh. There's not a single place I could scrape where I'd come up with that kind of cash."

"The judge said he normally doesn't issue bail for a first-degree murder charge, but because I had people to vouch for me, he gave me a chance." She snorted. "Although I'm not sure where he thinks I'm going to find a million bucks."

"He was a friend of Scoots, I assume?"

She shook her head. "No, Scoots called him a flaming bag of dog biscuits."

I rolled my eyes. "Sounds about right. She needs to work on her courtside manners. Who could it have been, then?"

She tugged at an invisible string on the scrunched-up sleeve of her jumpsuit and avoided making eye contact. "Judge Abernathy said it was somebody inside the station."

Gage.

I stared out the window toward the hallway. The blinds were open, and I could see Gage's office door was ajar. "You don't think…"

She folded her arms across her stomach and leaned back in her chair. "I don't want to talk about it."

"I'm going to figure out who did this," I assured her. "But you need to tell me everything."

Her foot scuffed the floor in front of her. "I'm not sure what's left to tell. Beau's dead. They think I did it."

I swallowed, then asked the one question I hadn't been brave enough to pose before. "Did you?"

Her nostrils flared, and she pegged me with a tired glare.

"I had to ask," I said. "But if you didn't do it, who did?"

She regarded me for a long time before finally responding. "I didn't kill him, Glory."

"I know—"

"But I did threaten to."

I reflected on the day before the murder when Josie had confronted Beau. Angry and hurt, she was full of foul-mouthed epithets about her ex-husband. "I remember. But you were in shock, and nobody blames you for reacting that way to seeing your ex-husband out of the blue after he flirted with another woman on national television."

"Look, Glory, I appreciate what you're trying to do, but I don't think—"

"You threatened to kill a man who wound up dead, and you're wearing an ankle monitor that puts you at the scene of the crime." I slammed my hand down on the table, making Josie jump and earning a side-eyed glance from the deputy. "You're my friend, Jo. And friends don't let each other go down for murder. So tell me everything that happened the day Beau died."

She took a stuttering breath. "I needed closure. And I didn't get that in the meeting Mimi set up."

"I understand," I replied. "She caught you off-guard, and you couldn't prepare. Not to mention the fact that you were practically in your underwear. Nobody envisions giving their retribution speech in a sports bra."

She acknowledged me with a grunt.

I leaned forward, resting my arms on the tops of my thighs. "You were near the warehouse when it happened. Did you see anything unusual?"

"You mean, other than the throng of people and the parade of emergency vehicles?" She ran her hand along the bulky cotton jumpsuit, smoothing out the wrinkles. "I don't think so. I tried to get as close as I could to the building, but there were too many spectators pushing and shoving. One man barreled out the warehouse door like a bowling ball, knocking people over all way through the parking lot. It was all I could do to jump out of the way before he flattened me."

I sat up straighter. "He came from inside, so he was part of the cast?"

"No, I don't think he's on the show."

"What did he look like?"

"He was a big guy, attractive. He had dark hair that stuck out all over the place." She fanned her face. "He was hot and kind of savage."

Rocco.

I rocked back in my chair. Why was the hairstylist in

such a hurry to flee the scene? Had he just dropped a chandelier on Beau?

~

AFTER I SAID goodbye to Josie, I stepped into the hallway to find Gage leaning against the wall just past the other guard, his blond hair shaggy and several days of beard growth casting shadows across his cheeks.

The top button on his uniform was undone, and it looked like he hadn't slept in a while.

He took a hesitant step forward when he caught my eye. "How is she?"

I nodded toward the visitation room. "Why don't you ask her yourself?"

"Because she won't talk to me."

"Even after you went to bat for her with the judge?" I asked.

"How did you know about that?"

A smug smile crossed my face. "Just a hunch. Listen, where do you guys stand on the investigation? Surely you've got other suspects."

He scrubbed his hand through his hair and studied the floor.

"You have other suspects, don't you?"

"You know I can't discuss this with you, Glory," he said.

I invaded his space and jabbed my pointer finger into his chest. "Listen to me." Jab. "Josie Lyons is a lot of things. Crazy. Impetuous. Far too reliant on crystals and her horoscope. But she is not a murderer." Jab.

Gage swept a gaze over my shoulder and lowered his voice. "Don't you think I know that?"

"Then why haven't you found out who really did this?" Jab.

He grabbed my hand, his grip firm and angry. "I'm working on it."

"It doesn't seem like it from here. From here it looks like you're standing back and watching a woman you care about go down for a murder she didn't commit."

"I'm following protocol. I don't want to lose my job."

I pulled my hand free. "Lose your job or lose the girl, Gage." Jab. "Your choice."

I SPENT the rest of the evening making a list of careers that would suit me better than wedding planning. I stared down at Rusty, who was curled up at my feet, a string of drool between his jaw and my sock, and added dog-sitter to the list.

Since I was brave and ready to try new things, I scratched out the word dog. If I could handle this hundred-pound beast and his predilection for stealing my underwear and eating most of my snacks, I could deal with a guinea pig or a potty-mouthed parrot.

I was just about to search online for pet sitting positions when a hesitant knock at the door sent Rusty into a barking fit. I stared at the clock. It was after ten, so it wasn't likely to be a social call.

When I peeked through the peephole, I found Josie wiggling her fingers in the air.

I threw open the door and engulfed her in a hug. "You're here," I said, pushing back to study her.

She smiled. "I'm here."

"But it's late... and you... how?" I stepped out onto the porch and glanced down toward the street. "Did somebody slip you a scarf so you could escape from jail?" I whispered.

"Didn't have to. Turns out I have a benefactor with deep pockets who paid for my freedom."

"Who?" I asked.

"I'm not sure. All I know is that Hollis pulled me out earlier tonight and gave me a stern talking-to about staying nearby and keeping myself out of trouble." She motioned toward her door. "And then they sent me home to wait for my court date."

"Somebody paid your bail?"

"It appears so."

"But who? Do you have any rich family members you weren't aware of?"

Josie shook her head. "No. I don't have anybody." She paused for a moment. "Unless you count a couple of creepy cousins from my mom's side, but last I heard, they were living on a goat farm in Texas and selling soap online. I doubt they even remember I exist."

She slipped the key from underneath her mat and unlocked the door. She hadn't been home in days, but when we stepped inside, every light in her apartment blazed brightly. Rusty gave an excited yip beside me and bounded toward the sofa.

Josie let out a soft gasp. "Scoots. What are you doing here?"

Scoots lifted a large plastic bag from the cushion next to her. "I have crabs."

I wrinkled my nose...

"Took you long enough to get here," she said, grabbing a bottle of champagne that had rolled into the gap between the cushions. "I posted your bail hours ago."

When I heard a sniffling sound from behind me, I turned to see Josie with the sleeve of her shirt balled up in her hands and tucked under her trembling lower lip. "You... you did?" she asked. "For me?"

Scoots glanced at me like she wondered if Josie had left her senses locked up in jail. "Of course I did. What's the good in having a fat bank account if you can't spend it getting your friends out of the slammer?" She stuck out the plastic bag. "But playing superhero makes me hungry, so I brought over something to eat. Do you like crabs?"

I tried to hide a grin. "It's not crab season, Scoots."

"Don't you think I know that, girl? These are from the freezer. It's not like you can get celebration food this late at night from the gas station. I had to improvise."

I took the bag and carried it to the kitchen. Sure enough, it was filled with breaded blue shell crabs. "What do you want me to do with these?" I called out to her.

The champagne cork popped, followed by the hiss of someone slurping up the bubbles. "Put them in the oven. I don't know for how long or at what temperature, so don't ask."

I knew better than to argue, so I fished through the cabinets for a sheet pan.

Scoots continued. "You can wait and ask Beverlee when she gets here in a few minutes. She's going to whip up some dill pickle tartar sauce to go with them." She turned to Josie. "Do you have the stuff for dill pickle tartar sauce?"

Josie laughed and put her arm around Scoots. "I didn't expect a party," she said over sniffles. "But I can't think of a better reason to have one."

Just then, Beverlee swept into the apartment without knocking, followed closely by Rusty, who sat down on the floor and stared up at the counter as if he were hoping a crab would leap into his open mouth.

Beverlee deposited a fat bouquet of black-eyed Susans from her garden on the counter with a flourish, their sunny yellow blossoms bright against the dark wood cabinets.

"Freedom flowers. Hopefully you'll stay out of jail long enough to enjoy them."

Scoots poured a healthy amount of champagne into four coffee mugs, then passed one out to each of us. "To freedom," she said. "And to finding out who did this."

We all toasted to that while Beverlee fussed about in the kitchen, chopping pickles and dill, and telling us about how Matilda had gone after the mailman. She held up the knife. "Oh, I forgot to tell you, Glory. Hollis got the official toxicology report back on your friend Caroline earlier tonight, and he was right—someone slipped something into her drink. Some kind of club drug. Poor thing was lucky it wasn't worse—a few more sips, and he said she would have gone into respiratory arrest."

I swallowed over the bubbles of champagne still lingering in my throat. "At least they can't try to pin that one on you," I told Josie.

"So, who can they pin it on?" Beverlee asked. "Who else was there for the party?"

"Unfortunately, most of the cast and a good portion of the crew," I replied. "It went from being a girls' night out to an on-location shoot pretty quickly. And Mimi is being shifty about letting me see the footage."

"Have you reviewed the backgrounds of the people on the show?" Josie asked, reaching into the drawer in the side of her coffee table to lift out her laptop. "Because I could use a project to distract me from everything else that's happening around here."

"Have at it," I said. "And start with Rocco. Something's going on with him and Lily, and he was there that night, looking particularly ferocious and intense."

After a few minutes of clicking her keyboard, alternating with shoveling food and champagne into her mouth, Josie's brow furrowed. "Did you know your guy has a record?"

"What kind of record?" I asked. "And he's not my guy."

"A couple of drug possession charges, and... whoa." She moved the laptop closer to her chest. "Three years ago, there was an incident where he was accused of stalking an up-and-coming Hollywood actress. He was arrested for possession of an illegal substance with intent to distribute it to a minor. It's all right here in the court documents for the entire world to see."

"And what happened?"

More clicking.

"Nothing," she said. "Charges just vanished. He was all over the news, and then he disappeared. Aside from a couple of low budget movies a few years back, he didn't show up in the press again until *Romance Revival*."

My chest tightened. "And just in time to commit a murder."

~

THE NEXT MORNING, after Shirley filled my mug and packed up a half dozen maple glazed donuts for me to snack on, I stopped by the police station to see Hollis. I found him sitting at a conference room table with a plate of fresh crab eggs Benedict and his own steaming cup of coffee.

I nodded toward the dish, a white ceramic plate with a bright blue ring. I had eaten waffles off those plates for years. "I'm glad I didn't get you a muffin. It would have seemed suspicious if both of us showed up with food this morning."

He rested his hand on his stomach. "I would tell you and your aunt that you need to come up with another way of trying to obtain information from me, but Beverlee is a superb cook, so I don't want to discourage her."

I cleared my throat.

"And you buy a great muffin."

I agreed with a dip of my chin.

"Can I assume this isn't a social call?" he asked.

I slid into a chair next to him. "Have you figured out who tried to hurt Caroline yet?"

"You know I can't discuss that with you, Glory."

I tilted my chin toward the stack of papers on the table next to his breakfast. "Can I ask if you've at least checked into somebody?"

He raised a brow but didn't speak.

"The hairstylist for the show. His name is Rocco Sabatino. It turns out he has a history of threatening behavior against women."

Hollis took a long sip of coffee. The only sound in the room was the liquid sloshing against the cup. "Go on."

"I think he might be in love with Lily Page."

"I've seen the Internet, Glory. Half the world might be in love with Lily Page."

"Yes, but he was there. He was there when Beau was killed and was also there the night that somebody spiked Caroline's drink."

"If he is so in love with Lily, why would he try to hurt her sister?"

I shifted in my seat. "I don't know," I finally answered. "It's possible Caroline was keeping Lily away from him."

He wiped his mouth with a napkin and pushed his chair back from the table with a scrape. "I love it when you visit, Glory, but trust me when I tell you we've got this under control."

A flush crept up my cheeks. "What about the footage?"

"What do you know about the footage?" he asked, deep furrows slashing across his forehead.

"Just that there was a camera crew there that night. They probably captured something that the rest of us weren't even aware of."

"We've considered it already," he said, transferring his gaze back to the papers. "And it was a dead end."

"What do you mean? They were filming the whole time. Surely they got a shot of the person who drugged Caroline. And once we know who that is, we—"

He held up his palm. "According to Mimi Wakefield, the camera went missing during the chaos. Without that footage, we've got nothing."

15

I stepped out onto my porch the next morning just in time to see Ian come to a stop on the street below me. He was wearing running shoes and his t-shirt was damp with sweat. I tried not to fan myself.

"It's too early for all that exercise, isn't it?" I called out, jogging down the steps toward the alley behind the pawnshop.

He shielded his eyes against the sun. "Shouldn't you have been at work an hour ago?"

"Funny," I replied, annoyed that he was right. I should have been down at the studio first thing this morning. Instead, I was sitting outside pretending I didn't want Ian to pull his shirt off to mop his sweaty brow. "I'm waiting for Scoots. I have a favor to ask her."

He chuckled and motioned for me to follow him toward the pawnshop's back entrance. He entered the code on the lockbox, a rush of cold air slapping me in the face as he pushed the door open.

"Why do I have a feeling this favor will end up with you in hot water?" he asked.

I shrugged and leaned against a filing cabinet. "Because you have no faith in me?"

His forehead wrinkled as he stared at me in silence. Finally, he raised a single eyebrow.

"Okay, fine," I huffed. "It might get me in a bit of trouble."

Just then, Scoots opened the office door with a loud smack, juggling a plate of chicken wings and a thick stack of mail. She studied us with narrowed eyes before sitting down at her desk. She pointed at the chicken, dripping with spicy sauce and a thick swirl of ranch dressing. "I had too much champagne last night. I needed sustenance."

I hid a smile behind my hand. "So, Scoots, I was wondering if you could help me with something."

Ian cleared his throat. "Don't do it, Scoots. She's trying to swindle an old lady into doing something that is probably illegal."

Scoots shoved her chair back with such force that it bounced against the wall behind her and rose to her full five-foot height. Although she was much shorter than Ian, when she puffed out like a rooster, she didn't seem so diminutive. "Watch your tone, son. Despite all of your bluster and those impressive biceps, I won't take attitude from the same kid who borrowed my Cadillac to try to get lucky at his first prom."

She took a bite of her chicken and pointed at him, then me, with the half-eaten bone. "Or his second."

I fought a flush as I remembered that night with Ian. It was the first time I had worn a fancy dress. The first time I had felt beautiful. Beverlee had spent the day fussing over me and pouring me into an emerald green satin shift with a slit up to my throat. When Ian saw me, his eyes had gone dark.

Kind of like they were right now.

Scoots dropped the chicken and smirked. "And if I

remember correctly, you were supposed to work off that little dent in my fender. You still owe me."

"What can I say?" Ian lifted his shoulder. "My date got handsy, and I didn't have the Caddy in park. If it wasn't for that telephone pole, I might have gotten lucky that night."

I glanced around for a quick escape from Ian's intense stare.

When the pawnshop's bell announced a new arrival, I released a whoosh of breath and leaned toward the hallway to see a middle-aged man in a suit unstrapping his watch at the front counter.

Scoots sat back down in her chair and crossed her arms in front of her chest, her cleavage rising almost to her chin. "Make it up to me, Ian. Go take care of my customer so I can help Glory break the law."

Ian contemplated the request for a moment before finally surrendering. He headed out front with the confident air of a man who still knew how to handle the job, even though it had been more than ten years since he'd worked behind the counter.

I felt certain he'd still know how to handle me, too.

Scoots kicked the door to the front of the shop closed and turned to me with a grin. "What illicit activity have you brought to my doorstep this morning?"

"Can I borrow your lock-picking kit?"

Without missing a beat, she shook her head. "No way."

"Why not?" I asked. "Surely there's a YouTube video I can watch to learn how to use it."

She shut me down with a glare. "If you need my kit, you need my skills. What are we breaking into today?"

"I need to get my hands on that footage."

"What footage?" Ian said from behind me. "Do I even want to know?"

I bit down on my lip. "You probably should. It has to do with your restaurant and what happened there."

"You mean besides a woman almost dying in my bar?" His fists opened and closed, and his nostrils flared. "Then, yes, I want to know."

I leaned back against the desk. "There was a film crew there that night, and there may be proof of somebody slipping drugs into Caroline's drink. But Mimi is being sketchy about the files."

"That seems like information the police would be interested in, doesn't it?"

"It does, but Hollis said they've hit a dead end," I replied. "I also think Mimi's hiding something."

"Like what?" Ian asked.

"Like the fact that her stylist, who is secretly in love with the bride-to-be, could have slipped a mickey into Caroline's drink, maybe to get her out of the way."

"Are you talking about that hairy Italian guy?"

I bobbed my head.

"He was stone-cold sober all night long. I thought he was security until somebody told me he was with the glamour squad. He never even came near the bar."

"Not that you saw," I suggested. "Maybe it happened while we were… outside."

He scrubbed his hand through his hair. "You think I was so caught up in you I didn't notice a killer in my bar?"

"Wouldn't be the first time." Scoots snickered from behind him before pivoting toward me with a wide grin. "Breaking into the producer's office sounds like a horrible idea. What time will you pick me up?"

～

WE WAITED until the sun started its descent into the water, the parking lot emptied, and the roving security guard made his rounds before we entered the warehouse. Mimi had given me a key card for the outer door so I could work overtime getting the set ready when they weren't shooting, so that at least gave us the illusion of not being criminal.

"Remember, if anybody asks, we're here to double-check the measurements for the stage," I whispered, holding out a measuring tape to back up my story.

Scoots nodded and adjusted her black T-shirt. She flashed me a thumbs-up like a geriatric pixie with a 40DDD bra and an attitude to match.

We had just taken the turn toward Mimi's office when disco music blared from the cell phone tucked inside Scoots's cleavage. She held up a finger in apology and reached down to silence the call.

After a few more steps, a text notification came in. First to her phone, then to mine.

I know you're in there. I see your car.

Scoots gaped at me with wide eyes. "I forgot to call Beverlee this afternoon."

I groaned and shoved my phone back into my pocket. "Go let her in," I said.

"No way. You do it. You're bigger than me. She'd have a harder time taking you down."

I grabbed her arm and tugged her toward the warehouse entrance. "Fine. We'll do it together. She can't kill both of us at once."

We made it to the door, and I threw it open to find Beverlee standing outside, arms crossed and high-heeled foot tapping on the gravel. "Please tell me you're not snooping."

"Snooping?" I asked. "Without you?"

Beverlee glanced at Scoots and let out a hoarse laugh.

"Might want to tell Darth Vader over there to go easy on the head-to-toe black next time. It makes her appear suspicious."

Scoots stepped forward, her eyes clenched into narrow slits. "This coming from the woman that wears a spandex unitard to buy peaches?"

"Fine," I said, shoving my way between the two women. "We're snooping. And you're going to get us caught. Get in here before somebody sees you."

Beverlee grinned and marched into the warehouse. "You're forgiven. What are we hunting for?"

I pointed toward Mimi's office. "We're trying to find the footage from Trolls the other night. Let's check the office first. If we don't locate it there, we'll hit the editing room."

"Do you even know what you're looking for?"

I shrugged. "No idea."

"And what will we do with it once we find it?"

"We'll figure out who is trying to kill people so we can get Josie off the hook, and I can finish planning this wedding in peace," I said.

Beverlee nodded once and led the way down the hall. "We need to hurry, then."

We stopped outside Mimi's office, and I extended my hand to Scoots like a surgeon getting ready to open up a chest cavity.

Scoots shook her head and pulled the lock-picking kit out of her hoodie's front pocket. "Not a chance. We all have our skills, and this is mine."

"Who are you kidding?" asked Beverlee. "You bought a DVD off a late-night infomercial on Court TV. It's not like you went to burglar school."

She huffed and reached for the doorknob. It turned in her hand. "Huh," she said. "That takes the fun out of things."

We walked into Mimi's office. A shiny chrome and glass

desk stood in the corner in stark contrast to the cheap accordion-fold plastic walls that created the space.

A tall vase of purple irises balanced on the desk next to a stack of papers and Mimi's clipboard. Her headset was charging on a table beside the small film-covered window.

Her laptop sat in the center of the desk, clamshell lid wide open, practically begging me to check it out.

My heartbeat whooshed in my ears, and as I strolled through toward the computer, dizziness swirled through my head. I steadied myself on the credenza.

"You need to carb up next time," Scoots said from behind me. She nudged me out of the way and swiped her finger across the track pad.

The screen came to life. No password required.

"Well, look at that," Scoots said with a grin. "It just turned right on. Nothing illegal about that."

I let out the breath I had been holding and dropped into Mimi's leather executive chair. Her computer screen was lit up with a still frame of Jason and Hazel embracing on the beach. When I pressed the space bar, the footage started to play.

My heart thumped again as I paged through the different folders, all named and labeled in descending order from the date the video was shot, and I said a silent prayer of thanks when Mimi's laptop was as organized as her ever-present clipboard.

I scrolled through the folders until I found the party at Trolls. "Bingo," I whispered. "The footage wasn't lost, after all."

Beverlee circled the desk and leaned down toward the computer. "Why would she lie about that?"

Suddenly, she lurched forward and hit pause. "Aha! I knew it."

My hand flew to my chest as I studied the screen. "What did you see?"

"You and Ian seem cozy," she said with a knowing smirk.

I groaned, tapping the play button again. "Not the time, Beverlee."

"What?" She lifted a shoulder. "I'm just saying there's enough heat flying off the two of you for all of us to enjoy a few s'mores."

I was about to tell her to go wait for us in the car when the camera shifted away from Ian and back to the bar. "Stop. We need to rewind."

We went back a few frames, and the three of us squinted at the screen. "Did you see something?" Scoots asked. The playback showed the group of us walking toward the bar and Ian setting out several drinks. The cameras followed us as we strolled into the room. The shot was smooth, as if the cameraman had stepped behind the bar himself.

"Ian won't let anybody behind that bar," I noted. "So how did the guy with the camera get back there?"

Scoots snickered. "Maybe our friendly neighborhood bartender was too distracted to notice somebody else in his airspace."

My flush turned to alarm when I heard Mimi's high-pitched voice coming down the hall.

"Get a grip, sunshine. The thing with Beau was unexpected, but it will benefit you in the end. Sympathy brings in the ratings."

"But I'm not sure I even want to go through with it anymore," a second voice said. "I can't relive the humiliation again and again."

Lily.

The voices stopped right outside Mimi's door, and panic shot through my chest. I quickly assessed the room for somewhere the three of us could hide. The window was too high to escape through, and I doubted we had that much time, anyway.

I took a deep breath and straightened my shoulders as I flung open the door and made a show of speaking over my shoulder. "I'm so sorry, ladies. I must have taken too long at dinner, but that tiramisu was worth the delay. I was hoping Mimi would still be here because I know you wanted to meet—"

I barreled out into the hallway and ran straight into Mimi, who was standing in the dead center of the hall, Lily frozen in place at her side.

"Oh, you're here," I said, my voice a full octave higher than normal. Fake enthusiasm was hard on the vocal cords.

Mimi's glare bounced between me and her door. "What were you doing in my office?"

"We were waiting for you. I wanted to hold back until the cast and crew had left for the day before I brought them in. You know," I whispered, peering down the hallway behind her. "Because of confidentiality."

Mimi continued to stare at me.

"Mimi Upchurch, I'd like to introduce you to your biggest fan. This is my aunt Beverlee and her friend, Scoots Gillsepie."

Beverlee's eyes widened momentarily, then she turned to Scoots with a big smile. "Oh, my. Isn't this wonderful?"

Scoots snapped her lips closed and mumbled a quick burst of profanity under her breath. "It's a dream come true."

"Beverlee is a huge fan," I said with a wide grin. "In fact, she has started a *Romance Revival* fan club," I said.

"I'm the president," Beverlee eagerly added.

Mimi narrowed her gaze and focused on Scoots, whose shoulders were trembling with repressed laughter. "What's your job, then?"

Scoots pulled a ballpoint pen out of her front pocket and clicked it several times. "Secretary," she replied.

Beverlee rushed forward and swept Mimi into a full-body hug, and when she danced backward, there were tears in her eyes. "It is such an honor to meet you, Ms. Upchurch. The work you're doing? It's so important."

Mimi seemed stunned. "It is?"

"Oh, yes," Beverlee gushed, grabbing her by the hand. "You're giving a voice to people who have made mistakes. You're the champion to those of us who think we don't deserve a second chance at love."

Beverlee turned to Lily, whose mouth had dropped wide open. "And you, dear," she said. "I do hope you'll be able to find happiness. You've been through so much. How's your sister?"

Lily's lower lip quivered before she manufactured a smile. "She's going to be okay, thank goodness."

"That's good. She had us scared there for a little while."

"I'm not sure my father will ever let her out of his sight again," she said with a terse laugh. "In fact, he's probably babysitting her back at the hotel as we speak, so I should—"

"Are they any closer to figuring out who did it?" Scoots asked.

Lily's smile dropped, and she stared at the floor. "I don't think so."

"Well, I hope they figure it out soon so you can focus on your wedding," Beverlee said, reaching out to wrap her arm around Lily's shoulder.

"No bride should have to worry about a murderer on her special day," I said.

Mimi cleared her throat. "We don't talk about murder when we have guests," she said with a glance that shot pointed beams of fire in my direction. "And it goes against the nondisclosure agreement you signed. But given the circumstances, and your aunt's obvious enthusiasm, I'm sure it was a simple oversight."

She turned to Beverlee. "Would you enjoy a tour of the studio?"

Beverlee beamed. "That would be wonderful if you have the time," she said, her Southern accent so thick she made it sound like wun-duh-fuhl. As she tugged Scoots down the hallway, she whooped and not-so-quietly whispered, "She is every bit as fabulous as I imagined."

The first genuine smile I had ever seen appeared on Mimi's face. "I'll do anything for my fan club."

16

As soon as I walked into the studio later the next morning, I knew making it out of the building unscathed the previous night didn't mean my luck would continue. Instead of showing up at the warehouse with my portfolio and a long list of ideas, I should have called in sick and stayed in my pajamas with a takeout order of blueberry waffles and an extra-large latte.

The sharp clang of metal on metal echoed through the building, followed by a head-splitting, high-pitched screech.

"What's going on?" I whispered to the cameraman as he scurried by with his chin down.

With a thin film of sweat on his forehead and terror flashing in his eyes, he glanced over his shoulder. "Mimi's on a rampage. Get out while you can."

I wrapped my arms around the stack of fabric samples I was carrying and turned back toward the entrance, but I didn't make it ten feet before I heard a loud thunk behind me.

Regretting that I hadn't been faster in my escape, I pivoted in slow motion.

Mimi stood with her palm against the wall, her eyes wild and tinged with red. Papers from her clipboard had rained over her shiny black pumps. "You." She pointed toward my chest. "Come with me."

After a quick glance around to make sure she was talking to me, I forced a smile. "Good morning, Mimi. Is everything okay?"

Her fingers curled over the doorframe. "Does it look like everything is okay?"

I made a gurgling sound.

She whirled to go back down the hall. "I need your help." She motioned toward all the pages scattered on the floor. "And pick those up."

I debated leaving her to her tantrum and the muddled pile of color-coordinated papers.

Publicity, I thought, inhaling to the count of ten. *You can't punch the woman who's going to give your company national exposure.*

"Of course." I scooped up the papers, hiding a satisfied grin as I shuffled them like a stack of cards, then shoved the clipboard under my armpit and hurried down the hall behind her.

We made it to the back of the warehouse to find Lily and Hazel seated in the hair and makeup area, barefaced and wrapped in white terrycloth robes.

"I need you to handle this." Mimi gestured toward the brides.

"I'm not sure what you—"

"Hair, Ms. Wells," she said with a glare. "Makeup. I need them camera-ready in less than an hour."

"Me? You want me to do that?" I hadn't washed my own hair in two days. I threw tinted moisturizer on my face on the way out the door that morning, and that was only because I was trying to hide a pimple caused by too much chocolate and too little sleep.

I scanned the mix of false eyelashes and curling wands spread out on tables in front of me and felt a jolt of alarm. "Where's Rocco?"

Mimi sighed, a dramatic hiss that dropped the temperature of the room by at least ten degrees. "If I knew where that no-good Italian hair gel freak was, do you think I'd be standing here right now?"

Lily and Hazel studied us with wide eyes, their mouths ajar.

"What about another stylist?" I asked. "Surely there's somebody—"

"You. There's you." Her gaze bored into me. She whipped out her phone and waved it in the air. "Or do you want me to call Magnolia?"

Maggie was probably the better choice. Even when I ran into her at the Food Barn on a random Sunday afternoon, she looked like she had just stepped off a runway or met with the queen. In my mind, though, there was something a little off about a person who wore a full face and kitten heels to pick up trash bags and frozen beef Stroganoff.

I might not know much about glamour, but I knew enough to keep Mimi from reaching out to my worst enemy with a neon sign that said I couldn't handle everything that came with the job. "No," I insisted. "I've got it. They'll be on the set in an hour."

Mimi stared at me for a moment before stomping over and yanking the clipboard out from underneath my arm. "I need them in evening wear," she said with a snarl.

It was only ten in the morning.

"Sure," I replied from between gritted teeth. "No problem."

~

THE SHARP BEAT of Mimi's shoes on the concrete floor hadn't even dissipated before I picked up my phone to call Beverlee. Fifteen minutes later, she showed up at the front desk with a designer rolling suitcase and a bright green tote bag printed with the Beverlee's Bites logo.

"Oh, this is fun," she exclaimed, wheeling what appeared to be the entire contents of her bathroom behind her down the hall.

"I was going to let them do their own makeup," I said as we turned the corner to the staging area. "I figure they're grown women. Surely they know what to do."

Beverlee stopped walking and turned to me with furrowed brows.

"Fine." I sighed. "Most women know what to do."

She pushed me aside. "It won't hurt them to have somebody else fix them up. It's like playing dress-up with life-sized dolls."

I used to pop the heads off my dolls and stick them in the microwave to see if their faces melted. Somehow I doubted that was what Beverlee had in mind, so I held out my arm to usher her into the room.

"Ladies," I said. "This is Beverlee. She's in charge of your hair and makeup until Rocco comes in."

While Beverlee got busy unpacking the equivalent of a department store cosmetics counter onto the table, I approached Lily. She was chewing on her nails and nervously watching the door.

"Have you heard from Rocco?" I asked.

She shook her head. "Not since yesterday," she replied, her bottom lip quivering. "And I'm worried."

"He could be running behind. Or he overslept." I shrugged. "You know how Italian men can be. He could have been out late last night partying with a troupe of redheaded circus performers."

"I don't think so, Glory," she said, fidgeting with the fabric of her robe. "He isn't the partying type."

I remembered the stories Josie had found online. I leaned in and whispered, "Are you sure about that? I thought he had quite a wild history."

She grabbed a tissue and rubbed underneath her eyes. When she peered up at me, the tissue was clenched in her fist. "He's not like that. Not anymore."

"People don't just change, Lily."

"He did," she said with a sharp nod and another glance at her phone. "What if something happened to him? Or…"

"Or what, dear?" Beverlee asked.

She took a wobbly breath. "He said he had feelings for me, but I turned him down. What if he left?"

"You should concentrate on one man at a time," Hazel supplied with a scowl. "I saw a picture on *The Enchanted Tattler* of the two of you cozied up on the beach. There's a whole comment thread about how you flit from man to man like a ridiculous floozy."

Lily brushed off her suggestion. "We're just friends. He has been helping me with something."

"That's what you're calling it these days?" Hazel snorted. "You really should be more careful. There are paparazzi all over the place."

"I know." Lily picked at a loose string on the front of her robe. "And that's the problem. They're so… invasive. One of them was even hiding in the bushes yesterday when I got back to the motel. It was terrifying."

"Isn't that what you signed up for?" Hazel suggested with a sneer. "You can't play innocent now, not after half the world saw your lap dance on YouTube."

Lily gasped. "I just want to make sure Rocco's okay, and

that one of those photographers didn't go too far and hurt him."

Lily's eyes were wide, and I put a gentle hand on her shoulder. "Let's get you ready, and I'll bet Rocco will stumble in here before filming starts."

With a tiny sniff, she agreed.

Beverlee stopped in front of Hazel, who appeared to be taking selfies in the makeup mirror. "This is going to be easy. Your skin is phenomenal, and I'm not sure how you got your hair so glossy, but I'm going to need you to write down the name of the products you use."

Hazel preened at her new fan.

Beverlee ran a finger down Hazel's pale cheek. "I once tried an octopus facial for fine lines. Those suction cups are supposed to increase blood flow, but all it did was make me look wrinkled with a bunch of hickeys on my face."

But when Hazel lifted a hand to give a disinterested yawn, Beverlee gasped and yanked it toward her. "You have mangled that manicure, though. Have you been dueling with rabid pirates?"

Beverlee dismissed Hazel's blank stare with a wave. "Never mind. We'll have you ready for the cameras in no time."

She spent the next forty-five minutes fluffing and curling the two brides-to-be, and by the time she was done, both Lily and Hazel were radiant and prepped for the cameras. Lily's tear-streaked cheeks had been smoothed and blended, and no signs remained of the emotional toll Rocco's absence had taken on her.

After they headed off to the set, I helped Beverlee pack her cosmetics back into the suitcase. "Don't you think it's odd for him to run off in the middle of filming?" I asked.

"Maybe he realized the police were getting close to

pinning the murder on him, so he took off while he still had the chance."

I nodded. "So far, all they have is circumstantial. Why would he run off today? He seemed fine the last time I saw him, not like somebody who thought the hammer of justice was about to come slamming down on him."

Tugging the suitcase's zipper closed, I turned to Beverlee. "Maybe we should go find him."

"Good luck," Mimi said from the doorway, her shoulder resting against the metal frame. "I've already sent a production assistant over to wake him up, but he didn't answer his door."

"Have you called the police?" I asked.

"To tell them what? That one of my low-life employees decided show business was too much, so he hit the road? Happens every day, sweetheart," Mimi replied, her voice mocking and full of spite.

She stared at me for a moment before pivoting toward the hallway. "If you can figure out a way to make a man stay when he doesn't want to, someday I'll be making a reality show about you."

After Mimi turned the corner, Beverlee leaned forward to ensure she had gone. "That woman is scary."

"But she could be right," I said, picking up the suitcase handle. "What if the stress of the show was too much for him, and he skipped town? He's probably down in Mexico rubbing guacamole all over unsuspecting tourist women by now."

"Avocado makes a nice emollient," Beverlee agreed.

My hands dropped to my sides, and the suitcase toppled to the floor in front of me.

"What?" She shrugged.

"There's only one way to know what happened to him," I

said. "We need to go back over to the Budget Motel and see if we can figure out where he went."

She plucked a bright pink brush from the tote bag and bent toward the mirror, teasing her bangs with practiced enthusiasm. "Okay, but can we stop off at Fat Hector's for some chips and salsa first? All that talk about guacamole made me hungry."

17

I fluttered my fingers at Jimbo as I drove past the security station into the parking lot of the Budget Inn. He had his nose tucked in a gossip magazine, and he waved us by without a second glance.

Beverlee sat beside me, swiping her finger through a Styrofoam cup of cheese dip.

"Do you want a spoon or something?" I asked. "Or are you going to drink it like a milkshake?"

"You're only grumpy because you're hungry. I saw a segment on Dr. Oz about it. They called it being hangry, and it means your blood sugar is low. You shouldn't try to solve a murder with low blood sugar."

My stomach grumbled. I couldn't argue with Dr. Oz. "Fine. Save me some. But let's get this out of the way first."

I stepped out of the car just as Zoey exited the registration office, pushing a rickety cart overflowing with cleaning supplies and balancing a mop and a bucket in her arms. She nodded as she barreled past me. "Sorry, I'd stop to chat, but our housekeeper got stuck at home with a barfing six-year-old, and I have an inn full of rooms to service. These TV folks are high maintenance."

I pointed at the car, watching Beverlee stuff a taco into her mouth. "No problem. But Beverlee and I need to drop something else off for Mr. Sabatino."

Zoey made a waving motion toward my Honda, big globs of water splatting the ground at her feet from the still-wet mop. "There's a second set of keys on a hook in the office. Swing them back by before you leave."

Nervous energy tugged at my belly when I reached behind the door and snagged the keys. On my way out, I made a beeline for the desk and quickly flipped through the guest cards to see where everybody else from the cast was staying.

I returned to the car just as Beverlee was wiping her face with a paper napkin. She gently folded it and stuck it in the takeout bag, then tucked the edges over twice and set it on the floorboard next to her feet.

She obviously hadn't seen the stash of balled up fast food trash up in the back seat.

I held up the keys. "Bingo. Let's go wake up our Italian lover boy."

I rode around to the side of the building and parked a few spaces down from the stairs. Like last time, the parking lot sat mostly empty, sprigs of grass breaking through the pavement to mask the parking lines. I noted Rocco's rental SUV next to a line of dandelions. "My guess is he's hungover and sleeping it off."

I glanced over my shoulder at Beverlee as she trudged up behind me. "Mimi's room is right next door," I whispered. "If we happen to get lost on the way back to the car."

"Those outdoor stairwells are often confusing," she said with a brisk nod. "Especially when you can see your car the entire time. But I suppose it wouldn't hurt to take a peek."

I knocked on Rocco's door.

No answer.

I knocked again, louder this time. "Housekeeping," I bellowed.

When he still didn't respond, I slipped the key into the lock. I pushed the door open and stepped inside, expecting to see the carpet covered in lacy red thongs and empty bottles of prosecco.

Instead, the room was immaculate, the coverlets crisply creased and the floor clear of debris. Even the veneer tabletop was spotless, free of the incriminating papers we found when we last paid him a visit.

"Not what I expected," I said as Beverlee dug through her purse with studied precision. "What are you searching for?"

She inclined her head toward the Magic Fingers box on the nightstand. "This time I brought change."

She slipped a coin into the box and grinned as she rested back on top of the covers. "Where else can you get a fifteen-minute massage for twenty-five cents? It's a bargain. They don't make beds like this anymore."

"And thank goodness for that," I muttered. Nothing sounded less appealing than a bed dancing the jitterbug in a motel whose slogan was "When you have nowhere else to go."

While Beverlee jiggled on the 40-year-old mattress, I inspected the room. The trash can sat empty, its plastic liner intact. There weren't any dirty needles or airplane bottles of liquor in sight.

A variety of vintage hair band t-shirts were folded neatly inside the dusty dresser drawers. "This is odd," I said. "Rocco's stuff is still here. He didn't leave town."

She gave a pulsating murmur that sounded like an acknowledgment, but her eyes were tightly closed.

I walked over to the bathroom. The door was closed but not latched. I kicked it open with my foot.

The Pepto-colored tile was dingy and cracked, and the hand-cranked window appeared rusted shut. Salt air had given the glass a hazy finish. The shower curtain, an aged light brown, was flecked with mildew that matched the tile. I gagged and fought the desire to wash my hands.

High-end hair and skin care products lined the edges of the vanity, their clean lines and modern colors the yin to the rest of the moth-eaten bathroom's dirty yang.

Just before I turned to leave the room, a roach the size of a small Buick crawled out from behind a pomade jar. I screamed and jumped back, grabbing the shower curtain to break my fall.

But instead of the cold, grimy tile I expected, my palm landed on a very tan, very hairy male leg.

I jerked the curtain all the way back.

Rocco Sabatino reclined in the tub, showing far too much Italian thigh, his eyes open and accusing and his hands frozen in a grip around the edges of the ceramic. Light gray foam clung to the corners of his mouth, and his skin was pale and splotchy.

He hadn't skipped town. He hadn't even left his room. Or put on pants.

I averted my eyes from the tightie-whitie-wearing corpse.

I scrambled out of the tub when I heard a screech from the bedroom. I bolted around the corner to find Beverlee, wildly bouncing up and down on the bed like she was riding on a mechanical bull. "Get on," she cried, her voice fluttering with the movement. "I think it might be broken, but this is amazing."

"Up." I pointed toward the exit. "We need to go."

She didn't listen. Instead, she spread her arms and legs out as if she was making snow angels on the mattress.

"Beverlee, it's Rocco. He's… we need to call the—"

"Police!" a loud voice boomed from the other side of the door. "Open up."

I took a deep breath and peeked out the window from behind the fungus-colored drapes. Hollis and Gage stood outside, weapons drawn.

Hollis raised a brow when I hesitantly opened the door, but then his gaze slipped past me to Beverlee, who was trying to sit up while the bed jerked back and forth. "Ladies," he drawled while surveying the room.

Beverlee smoothed down her shirt and brushed her hair behind her ear, her hair still undulating as she struggled to straighten her body. "Hello, Hollis. This is a pleasant surprise. What are you doing here?"

He slipped his gun back into the holster and held out his hand. She eagerly grasped it, and he hauled her to her feet. "I could ask you two the same thing."

"We came here to find the hairdresser," she replied. "He didn't show up to the set this morning, so we thought we'd come by and make sure he was okay. But he wasn't here."

I swallowed, acid burning the back of my throat. "Actually…"

Beverlee didn't slow down. "And we found this old bed and you know how I love that kind of thing."

Hollis flushed and dropped her hand.

"It seems like you're busy. We'll just be on our way," Beverlee said. "Hopefully, you can find Rocco. The girls looked beautiful this morning, but I'm not on staff with the show and I'm sure there are unions for that sort of—"

"He's… he's in the bathroom," I stuttered and pointed across the room. "And I think he's dead."

Beverlee shrieked and immediately hid behind me, using my body as a shield.

Hollis pulled out his weapon again and jerked his head

toward Gage. "Stay here," he instructed us, then motioned to the vibrating bed. "And turn that thing off before you kill someone else."

～

"I can't believe you let me rattle around on the bed like a piece of day-old popcorn when there was a dead man in the bathroom." Beverlee folded her arms and glared across my living room. "At least you could have told me before you opened the door for the police."

"I'm sorry," I said, dropping my head into my hands. "I tried, but it all happened so fast. I wasn't expecting to find anybody behind the curtain."

"Let me get this straight." Scoots chuckled, wiping tears from her eyes. "You found another body. In a dirty shower."

"It's not funny, Scoots." My stomach lurched as I remembered Rocco's vacant stare and the waxy tone of his skin against the filthy porcelain tub.

"If you're going to bite the bullet in your underwear in the middle of a roach motel, you've got to expect a snicker or two," she responded. "When it's my turn to go, it will be dramatic. Think skydiving accident over the Grand Canyon. Or throwing myself in front of a speeding train to save a baby in a stroller."

"Or choking on a churro in a gas station parking lot," Beverlee added with a smirk.

"That was one time," Scoots replied, her grimace quickly replaced with a well-timed hand gesture. "And it was hotter than I expected."

She fixed her scrutiny on me. "What happened while you were at the police station?"

Beverlee snorted. "Besides us having to stand there while

that black-haired girl from the television show complained she was getting too much attention?"

"We had to wait for Hazel to give her statement," I told Scoots. "Apparently, Lily's not the only cast member the paparazzi are hounding. Hazel is worried they're going to post unflattering pictures of her on one of the tabloid blogs."

"That's understandable," Beverlee agreed. "There's nothing worse than flipping open a magazine to discover a picture of your favorite celebrity in yesterday's makeup and hair that looks like a home for unwanted rodents."

"There are plenty of things worse than a bad photo on the Internet."

"Name one," she challenged. "War and starving children don't count."

I pinched the bridge of my nose. "We found a body today. And if that wasn't awful enough, we also had to sit through a fun round of questioning that resulted in them taking our fingerprints and plucking out strands of our hair."

Unfortunately, the Flat Falls police station now housed more information about my personal life than the computer system at my gynecologist's office.

"They took hair samples?" Scoots asked.

"They said it was standard procedure for people caught rutting around in a crime scene." I glanced at Beverlee, who was busy studying her fingernails.

"Did Hollis tell you what they were doing there to begin with?"

"Not really. Just that they had gotten a call to do a welfare check and jumped into action when they heard Beverlee screaming."

Scoots grinned. "That would do it. Nobody wants to overhear an old lady caterwauling on a vibrating bed. That's the stuff nightmares are made of."

Beverlee threw a pillow across the room, and it clipped

Scoots on the arm. "You're older than me," she said with a huff.

"Yes, but at least I'm subtle about it."

I cleared my throat. Scoots was about as subtle as an acute case of chickenpox.

"Focus. Our friend is still in trouble, and the only other person with a solid motive is dead," I replied. "On one hand, this helps to prove Josie's innocence."

"And on the other?" Scoots asked.

"There's still a killer out there, and any of us could be next."

THE SUN HADN'T EVEN COME up the next morning when I found myself seated on the bench outside the Grind and Go. I hadn't slept, and with a to-do list full of show prep ahead of me, getting my hands on the largest coffee Shirley could pour was imperative.

Dew still coated the metal and soaked through my thin cotton pants. I closed my eyes and inhaled, trying to find my center. Unfortunately, my center felt like I had wet myself.

When I heard heavy footsteps on the sidewalk, I jerked my head up, blood rushing through my ears with a deafening roar.

Instead of a barbaric convict with a plan to cut me into bite-sized chunks of bait, Ian jogged to a stop in front of me. He rested his hands on his thighs while he took in a few jagged breaths.

"You scared me," I said. "I thought you were here to commit another murder."

He raised a brow. "Another one?"

As I told him about finding Rocco's half-naked body in

the bathtub, not even Ian's exercise-warmed frame was enough to fend off the chills.

He sat next to me, throwing a steadying arm across the back of the bench. "First, there was Beau. Then somebody attacked Caroline. And now, Rocco."

Nausea swirled in my chest. I peeked at my phone to check the time, wondering why Shirley picked today to be late. I needed coffee and a biscuit, or I'd dry heave all over the sidewalk, hot man nearby or not.

"Do they have any more suspects?" he asked, his warm hand resting on my upper back.

"I haven't heard." I reclined into him like a cat, practically begging him to pet me. His touch was comforting. Strong. And not murdery.

He moved his fingertips in small, mesmerizing circles. "And Josie?"

I held back a groan at his touch. "Hollis still thinks she's responsible for Beau's death."

He leaned in close enough for me to smell the shampoo in his sweat-dampened hair. "And you don't?"

"No." I stood up before I started to purr. "But I can't figure out the missing link between the deaths."

"Start with the obvious. What's the one thing they all have in common?"

"They're dead. Or almost dead."

"Right. But beyond that."

I tilted my head toward him. "Lily Page, the Pickle Princess."

"America's second-chance sweetheart."

I studied the water as the first swirls of orange danced in the sky. Lily seemed to have everything going for her. The camera loved her, the show's fans adored her, and there was no shortage of men lining up to swoon at her feet. "But what if it's all an act?"

"What do you mean?"

"Don't you remember anything from high school history? Pirates used to light lanterns along the beaches here. Ship captains thought they were lighthouses, so they would steer their boats accordingly. By the time they realized the lights weren't real, they'd run aground, and the pirates would swoop in and steal everything."

He nodded. "Smart trick. But I don't see what this has to do with—"

I continued, my pulse thundering in my ears. "They called them false lights. Illusions."

"Lily does have a way with men," he said, understanding flashing in his eyes.

"She can have almost anyone, but the men she ends up with all have one thing in common—they have something she wants. When she turns the charm on, they sail right toward her. And then they crash."

"I hate to admit it, but you might be onto something. Some women just have a way of making men bang into themselves for them." Ian spoke softly, his gaze focused over the water.

I cleared my throat. "Big boobs and platinum hair?"

He chuckled and waved to Shirley, who was stumbling up the sidewalk balancing a basket of pastries and a box of fresh apples. "Doesn't hurt, I suppose, although I'm more of a leg man myself." He took a leisurely glance down my body. "And I like brunettes."

18

I spent the morning in a flurry of show prep that involved me peeking around every corner in the warehouse to make sure more bodies hadn't surfaced.

In two days, the winning couple would be announced on live television, immediately presented with a check for half a million dollars, and led down the aisle for their dream wedding. Shows with bigger budgets and more robust staff did that kind of thing all the time, only they had months to pull everything together. *Romance Revival* didn't have a hefty budget or a motivated crew.

If the morning meeting was any indication, most team members were one hostile leer away from either quitting or having a total breakdown. Everyone was jumpier than normal, and the lady from the front desk even hissed when the costume designer brushed past the back of her chair.

When Maggie wasn't scowling from her usual spot at the head of the table, I wondered if she had given up or at least encountered an ax-wielding assassin with a fondness for bad-tempered bottle blondes.

She strode in a few minutes later with a box of hot croissants, though, and I shoved one in my mouth to keep from showing my disappointment.

Not wanting to waste a minute on fresh pastries or homicide-related gossip, Mimi smacked her hand on the table and insisted everybody snap out of their anxiety.

"We don't have time for you to blather on about the demise of your coworkers," she said, forcing eye contact with each employee in the room. "We have more important things to deal with, like the mandate from finance to cut our production budget by ten percent. So, who wants an unpaid vacation?"

Several crew members shifted in their seats, clearly considering her offer.

When nobody spoke, Mimi lowered her chin and glanced in my direction. "All right, then. Wedding ladies, how do you propose we reduce our overhead?"

I rubbed my fingertip over a spot on the table until it glistened with croissant grease, which I tried to wipe off with my sleeve. "Um…"

"Speak up, Glenda," Mimi said. "There are no bad ideas."

Maggie snickered from across the table, and I gave her the stink eye before responding. "It's Glory. And how about we get rid of the ice sculpture?"

"No," Mimi exclaimed, slapping the empty chair beside to her with the back of her clipboard. "Bad idea. Next?"

Maggie leaned forward in her seat. "We could nix the doves. Not only are they expensive, but you risk them making a foul-smelling mess all over your pristine set, and I'm sure you don't want your expensive cameras covered in bird poop."

Mimi considered the suggestion for a moment before nodding her approval. "Done. Splendid job, Magnolia. Keep it up."

Croissant remnants roiled in my stomach.

Mimi's next order of business was to introduce a new stylist she had flown in on a red eye from Hollywood. Where Rocco was a towering fortress of Italian attitude and an impressive mane, the new one was a gangly woman with short purple hair and inch-long sparkly fingernails who clicked her dental appliance in and out of her mouth several times before she started each sentence.

"As you know, we have forty-eight hours until we shoot the ceremony," Mimi said as she tapped her watch. "That means you do nothing but work for the next two days."

I raised my hand tentatively. "Rocco was an important part of the *Romance Revival* family, and the crew is understandably upset about his... passing. Is there anything you'd like us to do to recognize him during the ceremony? A memorial, of sorts?"

Her clipboard clattered to the floor. "He kept me up last night, hollering at his television and banging around. The walls at the Budget Inn are as thin as the sheets. My job requires precision, and his noise level was unacceptable."

My jaw practically hit the table. "He was being murdered, Mimi. I think noise is part of the process."

She gave a disdainful grunt. "A memorial will not be necessary. I'm sure he has an actual family somewhere to take care of those details."

Before she stomped out to harass the stagehands, Mimi scooped up the box of croissants and dumped them in the trash.

By the time I gathered my things to head down to the ceremony set, a carb-starved production editor had slammed a cup of coffee down on the conference room table, splashing it on a keyboard and causing even more of a frenzy, and the new stylist had dashed for the bathroom in tears.

Maggie, however, seemed unaffected. When I stepped up

to the stage, she was on her knees placing vinyl planks in a herringbone pattern.

"I thought Mimi wanted actual wood," I said.

"That was before she saw the price tag. After that, I had to talk her out of slapping down a pile of animal-print bath-mats from Walmart and turning this into a safari."

I dropped my chin into my hands. "Are all weddings this hard?"

"Are you kidding me? Compared to some, this is a walk on the beach."

Grabbing a stack of vinyl, I sunk down next to her. I hoped the beaches Maggie strolled on were teeming with killer sharks and sinkholes filled with quicksand, because I couldn't imagine a wedding worse than this one.

ALTHOUGH I WAS SEARCHING for an excuse to sneak out of the warehouse that afternoon, when my pocket vibrated from an incoming voicemail, Beverlee's message had me fearing the worst.

"I need you, honey," she said, her breathing heavy and labored. "I'm down by the swings near the docks. Get here as soon as you can, it's urgent."

I tossed a shrink-wrapped box of tea lights on a chair and took off at a jog.

The Flat Falls waterfront district was only a few blocks long, but by the time I reached the common area, I was pant-ing. Sweat dripped down my forehead and stung my eyes.

I scanned the clearing where families played on checkered blankets underneath the shade of twisted live oaks and couples sat on old-fashioned porch swings arranged in a semi-circle facing the water.

Beverlee wasn't hard to spot. With a wide-brimmed pink

hat and matching swing dress, she appeared ready for Easter at the dance hall instead of a close call with the morgue. She balanced in the center of a swing, her arms overhead.

When she saw me approaching, she climbed down from the seat and waved. "Took you long enough," she said. "I'm getting too old to balance like that."

"You told me it was an emergency."

She pulled out a hand mirror, touching up the edges of her lipstick before folding it closed with a click. "It is an emergency, Glory."

I pursed my lips as I examined her. "You look fine."

She stepped back and twirled around, her ruffled skirt flying into the air high enough that a mother nearby covered her toddler's eyes. "Why, thank you," Beverlee said with a quick curtsy.

"You called me all the way out here in the middle of a workday so you could go fishing for compliments?" I kicked a patch of sand under the swing, oddly satisfied at the swirl of dirt that settled on Beverlee's espadrille sandals.

"I don't need compliments. What I need," she said, tapping me on the shoulder with the metal selfie stick she had been holding, "is someone to take my picture."

"Your picture?" I asked, squinting toward the sky for moral support.

"I met a man in an onion chat room online. He's smart and funny," she said, a hand resting on the crisp white bow stretched across the bodice of her dress. "And you don't know how hard it is to find someone who knows the difference between a Vidalia and a hole in the yard. I need you to take my picture so I can send it to him."

I held out my palm and tried to keep a straight face. "I'm not sure which is worse, a man who hangs out on an onion website, or a woman who dresses like a rockabilly waitress to impress him."

"All I want is a photograph, Glory Ann," she said, her hands on her hips and her voice taking the same disappointed tone she'd used when I got caught throwing her good toilet paper into the principal's trees when I was sixteen.

"You have this." I thrust the selfie stick toward her like I was trying to spear a hot dog. "Why do you need me?"

Groaning, she grabbed the stick from my hand and maneuvered it to face us. She ordered me to smile seconds before the shutter snapped.

After she unhooked the phone from its clamps, she pivoted the camera screen to face me. "When I hold my arm up to take my own picture," she said with an annoyed glare, "I get a boob wrinkle right down the center of my chest."

I took the phone from her outstretched hand and squinted toward the photo. "There's not a—"

"Nobody wants a boob wrinkle," she said emphatically, riffling through her oversized bag. "Especially not somebody trying to impress a gentleman."

"Beverlee, I'm sure the onion guy won't care about your—"

"Aha!" She wiggled a roll of clear tape in the air like a trophy. "All I need you to do is help me tape my décolleté and take a few snapshots. The lady at the makeup store said this stuff will defy gravity."

"I'm going back to work," I said, pointing to a picture of her smiling in front of the water. "Use this one."

She snatched the phone, slipping reading glasses out from the cleavage of her dress. Maybe if Beverlee stopped keeping household goods in her bra, she wouldn't have to worry about wrinkles.

She pushed it back toward me. "Not that one. My nostrils are too big."

I thumbed through several dozen pictures, pausing when

I hit the series of shots Beverlee took in the parking lot after Beau died. "Did you ever send these to Hollis?" I asked.

"No, I forgot all about them. Why?"

I pinched my fingers on the screen, blowing up an image of the crowd outside the warehouse. "I once heard that criminals like to hang out near their crime scenes so they can watch the chaos unfold."

"Makes sense. They want to witness their own power," Beverlee said, bringing her nose close to the phone as she squinted at the image. "Who do you see?"

My fingernail clicked as I tapped the picture to point out a familiar face. "Dan Nichols, who wasn't even supposed to be in town on the night Beau was murdered."

19

Chaos tailed me like it was attached to my rear end with hot glue for the few days before the wedding, but when I walked into the warehouse on the last morning of filming, everything was eerily calm.

Crew members sat on tufted sofas drinking sodas from glass bottles, their man buns and goatees still neatly groomed and not showing their usual level of anxiety-driven hair-pulling.

Soft rounds of laughter echoed against the faux wood walls that spanned both sides of the set, each one containing elaborate leaded glass windows lit from behind with light boxes. Rustic columns flanked the stage area, and metal buckets overflowed with fresh flowers and strands of twinkle lights along the aisle.

Globes filled with water and floating candles cast a warm glow, and a glittering, multi-tiered chandelier hung from a sturdy beam suspended between two high walls of scaffolding. I eyed it suspiciously and took the long way around, noticing most of the crew also giving it a wide berth.

Despite the drama that continued behind the scenes, it looked like a bridal magazine had come to life right there in Flat Falls, and I rolled my shoulders and felt several weeks of tension melt away.

We did it.

I stepped back to get a panoramic view of the set and almost tripped over Maggie, who was on her knees at the edge of the walkway, rolling a cream-colored raw silk runner down the aisle.

"I wasn't sure we could pull this off," I said, a satisfied smile tugging at my lips.

She stood and brushed invisible dust off the front of her gray slacks. "It's nice of you to join us this morning," she replied, her lips pinched together in the same mocking line she had flaunted when she won the sixth-grade spelling bee after I got kicked out for misspelling banana in the first round.

I glanced down at my watch, the sting of reproach tying my desire to introduce her perfect chignon to the contents of my still-warm travel mug of hazelnut coffee. "It's seven o'clock, Maggie."

She let out an unladylike snort. "Exactly."

I stood there in stunned silence until a frenzy fell over the room announcing Mimi's arrival.

Like a demonic tornado, the threat of her presence sucked every bit of peace out of the room. Crew members scrambled behind the walls with hushed curses, and Maggie crouched back on the ground to continue rolling out the silk as if she hadn't been about to stab my eyeballs with her stack of fabric pins.

Mimi strolled onto the set and halted in front of us. She gave the runner a cursory glance before her gaze dropped to her clipboard. "We shoot at eleven, and sixty guests will arrive by bus at ten. Make sure you're ready."

I pointed toward the lines of wooden benches inter-spersed with spindle-backed chairs facing the altar. We had planned to use the seating for the ceremony and remove it for the party afterward. "Are we still putting the brides' fami-lies on the left and the grooms' on the right?"

"Yes," she said with a stiff nod. "And seat the most attrac-tive ones on the aisles. Nobody wants to see Great Aunt Edna and her chin hair problem in high definition in their living rooms."

"But don't you worry about fighting?" I asked, an icy pool of dread forming at the thought of wedding violence. "Wouldn't it make more sense to put both Lily and Dan's guests on one side and Hazel and Jason's on the other? People might throw chairs when they find out their loved one lost."

A flash of satisfaction crossed Mimi's face. "Now you're getting it. We need as much action as we can create."

I waved toward the stage. "So you're trying to manufac-ture pandemonium?"

"Our viewers want sparks, they don't want reality," she replied. "Reality is boring. Nobody wants to watch you brushing your teeth unless you're doing it in a teddy with your married plastic surgeon."

I cleared my throat and caught Maggie's wide-eyed glance. "We'll keep the families of both brides and both grooms together on opposite sides of the aisle."

Mimi focused on her clipboard. "Lily and Hazel will be here any minute, and we need to film you planning the ceremony."

"Don't you think it's a bit late to—"

She cut me down with a glare. "Footage. I realize you have already planned the wedding, but we need more footage of you discussing the plans with each bride."

"Got it," I said, pretending to straighten the piece of silk.

"And see what kind of dirt you can dig up, too," Mimi

continued. "I want them wistful about their exes while you're pinning on their veils. Bring up their daddy issues. Flaunt their humiliation. Remind them of the dead body. Whatever you have to do. Oh, and if you get me some tears, I'll throw in a bonus at the end of filming."

Beverlee was a wedding crier, so I had been down plenty of tear-filled aisles over the years. But I had never been asked to make a bride cry. Before I could clarify the instructions, Mimi had disappeared down the hallway.

I turned to find Maggie clutching her pearls.

"You heard the lady," I instructed with a nod toward the dressing area. "Let's go make a bride blubber."

I WAS HUMMING "THE WEDDING MARCH" when Maggie and I joined the brides in the makeup chairs a few minutes later. Stylists flitted around them like anxious birds, while camera crews dodged hot styling tools and thick streams of coconut-scented hair spray.

Mimi wanted both brides dressed in their wedding gowns when they announced the winners. They would escort the losing bride off stage, dry-heaving and with mascara streaming down her face, while the winner was whisked away for her fairy tale walk down the aisle.

"The photographers are waiting to get promo shots of you both before we start filming," Mimi said, not even bothering to raise her head from the notes in her hand. "That means no food or drink. We don't want to have to Photoshop your mouth because you couldn't resist a pre-announcement granola bar."

My stomach growled, and I interjected, "Actually, I like to make sure my clients eat something before their events. It keeps them from getting woozy under the blazing lights."

Mimi's head jerked up, and she speared me with a glare. "That's why they have grooms, Gladys. To catch them if they pass out."

I didn't even argue.

She zeroed in on Lily and Hazel. "Ladies, if you plan on fainting, please face the camera. No one wants to see your backsides like big, lumpy marshmallows if you fall the wrong way."

Lily's hand flew to her chest, and I gave her shoulder a reassuring pat. "If you get dizzy, loosen up your knees and take a deep breath. It will usually fade. Now, are you ready to greet your groom-to-be?"

"Isn't it bad luck for the groom to see the bride before the ceremony?" Lily grew paler with every passing minute. The way she was heading, she'd pass out before she even left the makeup chair.

Mimi scoffed, tapping her wrist to prompt the stylists to finish their preparations. "You're getting married on a reality television show to a man who disgraced you. For money. Bad luck is the least of your worries."

Hazel stared at Lily in the mirror. "It won't be bad luck when I walk away with half a million dollars tonight," she said flatly, her eyes snapping back to the fashion magazine spread out in her lap.

I jostled my way between the two women. "Easy, now. We need to keep your makeup intact for the camera. And despite what Mimi has said previously, nobody wants to see you claw each other's eyeballs out on national television."

I turned away before they could call me out on my lie. Everybody knew a catfight in wedding gowns was sure to deliver ratings.

With a soft sigh, Lily swiveled her chair to face the mirror. "I miss Rocco."

"I know," I said, scanning my brain for comforting

words, but coming up short. "It's always hard to lose a friend."

Her voice dropped to a whisper. "He was... more than that."

I flashed back to the stack of printouts that had gone missing from the table in his hotel room. "I know you were close, but how well did you really know him?" I asked tentatively.

"What are you implying?" Hazel barked from across the room. "That Rocco was a no-good loser, and the world is better off without him?"

Before I could stop her, Lily shot up from the chair and hurtled herself across the floor, a round brush still tangled in her hair. "What are you talking about? He was a kind, gentle—"

"He was a deadbeat with a history of hurting women," Hazel said with a derisive scoff. "Everybody knew that."

Lily's eyes blazed, and she wagged a finger inches from Hazel's eye. "You don't know what you're saying."

I reached out a comforting hand. "Lily, I'm not sure how to tell you this, but there was something else going on with Rocco."

She spun around to face me. "What?"

I exhaled slowly. "I know you felt a special connection with him, but his feelings for you might have been more of an... obsession. He had a full stack of printouts of you in his hotel room. Pictures. Tabloid stories. Really personal stuff."

Instead of reacting with shock, Lily slapped her hand across her chest and let out a wheezy laugh. "You think..."

"I'm sorry, but he appeared to be stalking you," I whispered.

She hiccupped, her chest rising and falling in pants as she tried to control her laughter. She crossed the room and tugged open her tote bag, lifting out a familiar stack of paper. "These papers? Who do you think he got them from?"

I stared at her, noting her lack of surprise. "You? But why?"

"Because that stupid blog, *The Enchanted Tattler*, keeps doing stories about me," she replied, fanning the papers in the air. "And the stories are getting more and more aggressive. Yesterday's post all but accused me of murdering Beau in a plot to gain pity votes for the show."

"What did Rocco have to do with the stories?"

"He was trying to help me stop them," she said. "He wasn't stalking me; he was helping me."

"And he wasn't jealous you were marrying another man?" I asked.

She shook her head and gave a sad smile. "He was happy for me."

"Then he would have wanted us to pamper you today," I replied.

The new stylist led Lily back to the chair and untangled the brush, finishing Lily's preparation by winding sections of her long hair around a curling wand. "We're going with a corn-fed bohemian vibe for you. Prairie nymph meets Tinkerbell, right? Where's your veil?"

"She's not wearing a veil," I said. "Just a crown of wild-flowers."

I opened the pale pink box the florist had delivered earlier and picked up the delicate halo of small yellow flowers. "You'll be a beautiful bride. Rocco would approve," I said, a lump forming in my throat.

Lily's lower lip quivered, and she brought her fisted hand to her mouth. "Yes, he would. Because it's my wedding day," she whispered.

Hazel's brows shot up, and she fixed a menacing stare on

Lily. "Don't get ahead of yourself, Barbie. The day's not over yet."

20

After Lily and Hazel were zipped into layers of beaded lace and organza, I stepped onto the ceremony set. If I squinted past the cameras and lights, the metal scaffolding, and the fuzzy microphones dangling from thin wires, it could pass for any bride's dream wedding.

Subdued music wafted from the speakers as crew members escorted guests to their respective sides of the stage.

It was easy to pick out Hazel's friends, with their stick-straight hair, glossy fuchsia lips, and tailored black dresses with hems just shy of obscene. They took selfies with cell phones they weren't supposed to have and wore practiced expressions that said *Romance Revival* was beneath them. They were bored and beautiful.

Lily's guests, on the other hand, seemed delighted to be there. They smiled when they saw me and asked how they could help. They ran sun-worn fingers along strands of white lights and blotted away tears when they visited the table with photos of Lily's late mother, who she had wanted to be a part of the ceremony.

ERIN SCOGGINS

"You did an exquisite job," Beverlee said from behind me.

I turned with a gasp. "Beverlee, what are you doing here?"

"They think I'm your assistant," she whispered. She smoothed her hands down the seams of her A-line dress, a vivid pink get-up embroidered with lime green frogs. She hefted the enormous matching purse onto her shoulder before acknowledging the crowd. "And besides, this is the most exciting thing that has happened around Flat Falls since my last wedding. I wouldn't miss it for anything."

The music came to a sudden halt when Mimi stepped to the stage. Her high-necked black suit looked more like it belonged on an aged schoolmarm or a funeral director than it did a Hollywood producer. "Ladies and gentlemen," she began, her lips pursed as she surveyed the room. "Please take your seats, and we'll start soon."

A murmur spread through the crowd, and guests arranged themselves in flattering positions in front of the cameras. A woman who could have been Hazel's sister sat at the edge of her chair, long limbs twined around each other and cheeks pulled in so hard I worried she was going to suck up her entire body and disappear altogether.

"Show time," I said to Beverlee, motioning to an area toward the back of the room where we could watch everything unfold.

She clapped and followed me down the aisle, her floor-length green chiffon scarf fluttering as she walked.

Just before we got there, I glanced off to the side of the set. Hazel stood there, stick-still and regal, surveying the crowd with a cool gaze. She wore a sleek white column dress with her dark hair pulled off her face in an elegant chignon.

The pointed toe of her shiny platform sandal tapped a

steady beat against the wood floor as she turned and glared at Jason, who was standing next to her in a fitted black tuxedo.

"Uh oh," I muttered to Beverlee. "I need to take care of a pre-marital tantrum."

I stepped over to the couple with my palms raised, frantically searching for Maggie, who was nowhere to be found. "Hey, guys," I said in the same soothing voice I used with toddlers and telemarketers. "Having pre-wedding jitters?"

Jason's hand trembled as he smoothed his tie. "I'm not sure what I did. I told her she looked beautiful, and she said if I didn't get my act together, she would break up with me on national television."

Hazel glanced away for a moment. When she returned her focus to Jason, her expression was grim. "You said I looked nice. Nice."

Jason's face showed a flash of desperation, his clean-shaven cheeks draining of their normal tan. "And? You *do* look nice."

Hazel huffed. "You said I looked nice right after you spent thirty seconds eye-fondling little miss perfect over there."

Jason's gaze fell toward his scuffed loaner shoes, and I followed Hazel's finger until Lily came into view. Unlike Hazel, she stood alone, her long hair loose and wavy. She wore a simple empire waist gown with delicate beading, slim spaghetti straps, and a flowing confection of white tulle that brushed the floor.

Hazel saw me studying her and scowled.

I sprang into action. "You're stunning, Hazel. A bridal vision. The camera is going to love you."

I caught Jason's eye and swung my glance back over at Hazel.

He got the hint and cleared his throat. "The most beautiful woman I've ever seen," he said.

A quick flash of insecurity crossed Hazel's face. "Then why were you staring at her?" she asked.

Jason's Adam's apple bobbed. "I wasn't—"

"I mean, look at her. She's ordinary," Hazel continued, the slight tremble in her voice giving way to shrill accusation. "Why does she get all the attention? It's always about Lily. Even on that stupid tabloid blog, all they do is post stories about her. What does she have that I don't?"

Jason stared at me in alarm.

I shook my head slightly and rested my palm on Hazel's arm to calm her down, but even her skin was cold. I fought the urge to recoil. "Nothing," I assured her. "You're just different, that's all."

She eyed my hand as if it were made of refrigerated pig guts and jerked herself free. "Different how?" she asked, her tone spiteful. "Daddy's little girl has deep pockets and hair like a fairytale princess. And that's not me, is that what you're saying?"

Well, yes, I thought, but I shook my head, anyway. "No, not at all," I assured her.

I breathed a sigh of relief when Mimi appeared at the front of the set and commanded everybody's attention. "Let's begin."

I smiled and waved toward Mimi. "It's time to see if you're getting married today."

BOTH BRIDES STOOD on-stage as Mimi barked orders at the photographer.

Lily looked as if bluebirds were about to land on her outstretched palms. Hazel seemed like she wanted to hand-feed Lily a poisoned apple.

Mimi smacked her clipboard on the wooden podium and

nodded toward Jason. "You. Up here," she said and pointed to a small piece of tape on the stage next to Hazel.

She glanced around, her narrowed eyes surveying the crowd. "Where's Dan?"

A murmur swept over the room as everyone searched for the absentee groom.

My stomach rolled, and I wondered if it was unusual for wedding planners to back out of weddings at the last minute.

Mimi stepped forward, her fingertips white from clenching her clipboard. Her frantic gaze landed on me. "Where, exactly, is our second groom, Ms. Wells?"

"Just going to find him now," I said with a half-hearted wave, and then bolted out the rear entrance of the set.

Maggie met me outside. "Do you know where Dan is?" she asked, pausing to smile at Lily's third cousin, who was eavesdropping without shame from the back row. She grabbed my wrist and spun me away from the crowd. "Because if you lost the groom, the whole world will find out."

"I haven't lost the groom," I whispered, then squinted over my shoulder at the throng gathered expectantly near the stage. "At least I hope not."

I strolled through the set until I was out of view, then immediately scrambled through the rest of the building, flinging open doors and calling his name. If Dan Nichols was hiding in a random closet under a supply of moth-eaten shipping blankets, I was determined to find him.

I had almost given up hope he was in the warehouse when I saw him at the entrance, pushing his way past the security guard.

Dan ignored him and stumbled toward me, his rumpled dress shirt half-open and bunched around his waist. Stubble dotted his cheeks, and his eyes were ringed with red. I darted forward and looped my arm through his. "Nice of you to show up to your own wedding."

Dan raked his free hand through his hair and halted. "She doesn't love me," he mumbled.

I tugged on his arm, but he brushed me off. "She's still here, isn't she? Standing up there in a fluffy white dress waiting for you. It's time to go get married."

"But she's never going to forgive me," he responded with a despondent moan.

I scanned the hallway in a panic. Surely somebody else would come along and convince this man to walk down the hall to marry a fairy princess.

Unfortunately, the corridor was empty, so the job of resolving Dan's mental breakdown fell squarely on me.

But I couldn't just let him off the hook and pretend everything was fine. If I was going to convince him to marry Lily, then I needed to make sure he was in it for the right reasons.

There were enough brokenhearted women out there who had been duped by their husbands for me to knowingly add to the mix.

"You left her to face the humiliation after the video, then swooped to pick up the pieces of her heart after Beau died. As far as romance tactics go, your approach could use some work."

"I heard about Beau dying, and I jumped on the opportunity," he insisted. "I thought it might be my only shot."

"You had the chance to be a stand-up guy, but you chose the money instead," I said with an annoyed grunt. "That goes against the honorable man code. It's the first commandment, isn't it? Thou shalt not dump the woman you love in order to receive a pile of cash. Makes you look like a chump."

He slouched against the wall, and I debated whether to

encourage him or smack him on the side of the head with a giant palm frond from the receptionist's desk.

"Is that why you were in Flat Falls when Beau was murdered?"

His head jerked up. "What are you talking about?"

"We have pictures of you outside the warehouse the afternoon Beau was killed," I said. "But according to the producers, you didn't even get here until later the following day. So why were you here?"

"I already discussed this with the cops." He finished his slow drop to the floor. "I came to see Lily. I wanted to apologize and to ask for her forgiveness."

"And did you speak with her?"

"No. When I pulled into the parking lot, there were police officers all around and the area was blocked off. Beau was already dead."

I glanced down the hallway again. If I couldn't get him to that wedding soon, the whole thing would be canceled, and my fledgling business would be the subject of national ridicule. I pasted on a smile and gave his shoulder a few gentle pats. "You've got your second chance. What's stopping you?"

"After the video came out, my father gave me an ultimatum. It was her or my inheritance." His voice trembled. "I'm not sure I can choose between Lily and my family."

"You can, and you will," I replied, pointing down the corridor. "Right at this very moment, a lovely woman in a wedding dress is sitting by herself in front of a bunch of cameras, and she's counting on you."

My stomach twisted at the thought of causing a rift between Dan and his family, but just as I was about to give in and usher him back to the parking lot, Mimi came storming down the hall, headset in hand.

"You're here!" She scanned his body from head to toe, her

nose wrinkled. "But why do you look like you've been on a three-week bender in the bottom of a dumpster? I thought you were a respectable businessman."

Wide-eyed, he glanced at me, then back at Mimi. "I…"

She waved her hand in the air. "Never mind. I don't have time for stories. What I barely have time for is getting you in the makeup chair for some eye drops and concealer. We'll have to go with the lovesick and homeless mood."

"Mimi," I interjected. "I don't think—"

"And that's a good thing. I don't pay you to think. I pay you to act. And I'd like you to act like a wedding planner and go find Mr. Nichols a breath mint and a tie. There's one hanging behind the door in my office."

She whipped a set of keys out of her pocket and tossed them to me before dragging a dumbfounded Dan down the corridor. At the corner, she whirled around to face me. "And Ms. Wells?"

"Yes?"

Her scowl was clear despite the darkened hallway. "Don't forget. I can make you appear as good or bad as I want. If I don't get this wedding started soon, I'll make sure the world knows it was your fault."

I ROLLED my shoulders and gave myself a mental pep talk before setting off down the hall to find fresh clothes Dan could wear to his wedding. When I arrived at Mimi's office, I slipped in the key and opened the door.

A men's dress shirt with a blue striped tie hung on a hook behind the door, still wrapped in plastic from the dry cleaner. I picked it up and started to leave, but when I heard the rustle of fabric on the floor behind Mimi's desk, my throat went dry.

I took a hesitant step forward, freezing when a head popped up from behind the chair. I instantly recognized the poof of red hair and the black hoodie.

"Paparazzi aren't allowed in here," I said, lunging for the desk phone. "I'm going to call security."

Instead of making a run for it, he stepped around the desk and stuck out his hand. "Name's Jeff. I'm with *The Enchanted Tattler.*"

I hesitantly shook it, shooting an uncertain glance toward the door. "Okay, Jeff. This is private property, and you need to leave."

He crossed his arms and leaned back on the desk. "Actually, I don't. I'm an invited guest."

"Seriously?" I asked with an incredulous snort. "Who invited you?"

He didn't have time to respond because Beverlee chose that moment to throw open the door to Mimi's office. "Glory," she said in an exaggerated whisper. "Are you in here?"

"Right here," I replied, eyeing the man who was changing his camera lens on Mimi's desk.

Beverlee sashayed past us and tossed her oversized pink and green purse onto Mimi's chair. "I'm glad I found you. Everybody's getting restless out there. Lily's grandmother is passing out pretzels from her pocket, but I'm not sure how long she can hold them off."

Jeff dropped the camera into a messenger bag on his hip. "That's my cue, then." He gave a mock salute and strode out the door, closing it behind him with a soft click.

"Who was that?" Beverlee asked.

"Jeff. One of the photographers who has been following Lily and Hazel."

"What was he doing in Mimi's office?"

"It looked like he was snooping through her drawers. Said he was a wedding guest."

"Huh," she replied. "They'll let just about anybody in these days."

"Why do you think he was here?" I asked. "And who could have invited—"

I had just reached over to retrieve the shirt and tie off the back of Mimi's door when Beverlee's tote made a strange, high-pitched clucking sound. "What is in your purse?" I demanded.

Beverlee glanced down at the bag, not alarmed at all that it was sashaying across the leather seat. "It's Matilda. I had a custom tote made for her. I figured if all those fancy ladies can carry around their little appetizer dogs in swanky designer purses, I could do the same thing with my pet chicken."

My mouth fell open.

"It has a zipper and special panels to allow for ventilation. It's even waterproof. Want to feel?" She nudged the bag toward me with her foot. It was wiggling.

"You can't bring a chicken to a wedding, Beverlee."

Beverlee scoffed. "You obviously never met my second husband."

"Find a place to stash her until the ceremony is over. I'm not kidding," I said, pinching the bridge of my nose between my fingers with enough force to be classified as a do-it-yourself nose job.

I was interrupted by Mimi's high-pitched voice coming down the hall.

"How hard is it to find a tie? It's a tie, not Jimmy Hoffa's body," she screeched. "Where is Gloria?"

"You can leave Matilda in one of the supply rooms until the ceremony is over. She'll be fine."

Beverlee nodded her agreement, and I stepped toward the door. I threw it open as Mimi came to a stop in front of me.

With trembling fingers, I dangled her keys and the tie. "I'm sorry for the delay, but I had to—"

I searched the room for an excuse, my gaze finally landing on the restroom across the hall. "Wedding days always give me a nervous stomach." I leaned in and whispered, "Not something event planners like to admit, by the way."

Mimi gaped at me, her eyes wide. Leave it to bowel issues to cut a conversation short.

I grabbed her by the arm and swung her in the direction of the ceremony. I tugged the door shut behind me and hoped Beverlee could figure out how to hide her chicken and make it back to the set without getting caught by a killer.

21

Trying to quiet the guests' restlessness, Mimi directed the sound technician to exchange the upbeat instrumental music that had been streaming throughout the morning for a morose dirge combining bagpipes and an out-of-tune organ.

By the time we got Dan cleaned up and back on stage, half the audience was asleep, and at least two people had ripped the stuffing out of the seat cushions to shove in their ears to block the noise.

Mimi gave a shrill whistle to let everyone know the ceremony was about to begin, and I wondered if it would be tacky to rip off a section of upholstery to protect my own eardrums.

Dan shuffled back and forth on the balls of his feet next to Lily.

When Lily offered him a shy smile, he didn't respond, and she glanced out to the front row. Caroline gave her an optimistic thumbs-up.

I stood off to the side to watch the spectacle unfold. The director motioned for the camera crew to start filming, and as the show's host stepped forward, a hush fell over the crowd.

"Good evening. I am Javier McMasters, and I am excited to welcome you to what promises to be the night of a lifetime."

With his ruffled shirt tucked into tight black tuxedo pants and a violet crushed velvet blazer straining at the buttons over his ample belly, Javier appeared ready to officiate a go-go dancer's Vegas wedding.

Hazel cast a scornful glance at Lily before turning to face Jason.

He didn't return her eye contact. Instead, he rocked back on his heels and studied the crowd, a frown pinching his lips into a tight line.

Dan swayed slightly as he rested his hand on his stomach, his fingers clenching the now-wrinkled fabric of the borrowed shirt.

I scanned the room for a bucket. Nobody wanted to witness a vomiting groom.

Javier stepped toward the camera. "We started with ten men and ten women, each one faced with the challenge of learning to move forward given their past mistakes. They are rabble-rousers and mistake-makers, schemers and dreamers who were searching for redemption and romance."

He gestured at the group gathered in front of him. "America, you have watched as they worked through their pasts and readied themselves for amazing futures. And you have helped narrow down who you think is the most deserving of a second chance at love."

Applause filled through the room.

Javier continued. "We started with twenty, and now we are left with four. Two couples, matched with each other based on a series of psychological tests and physical challenges, each excited to take the next step toward their happily ever after.

"Tonight, one of these couples will win the wedding of a lifetime and half a million dollars in prize money to embark on their new life together." He swept his arm out toward the camera. "Are you ready to meet the *Romance Revival* champions?"

A few whoops of encouragement filtered up from the audience.

"Very well, then. Let's start with a look back at each of our challengers."

A big screen behind the contestants lit up with video of Hazel rushing through a wall of paparazzi, shielding her hand in front of her face against the bright lights and intrusive cameras.

That image was replaced with tabloid footage of Jason at a press conference forfeiting his surfing championships, his floral board shorts low on his hips and an ample amount of tanned bicep on display.

When the montage of their humiliating slip-ups concluded, all four contestants were staring at their feet.

"Jason and Hazel," Javier began, gesturing to each couple. "And Dan and Lily. Please step forward."

The contestants moved to the front of the stage. Jason took Hazel's hand.

Javier held out an envelope. "In this envelope, I have the results. Over sixteen million people cast their votes, and it was one of the closest contests in reality television history."

He slipped his finger behind the seal and tore the paper.

A hush fell over the crowd. Mimi clutched her clipboard and stared on in rapt attention.

"And the winner is…"

"Wait." Jason dropped Hazel's hand and dipped his chin toward the audience in apology. "I can't do this."

"Jason," Hazel warned, her voice icy. "Not now."

He shook his head, blond hair flopping over his brows. He focused on Hazel before raising both hands in the air in a signal of defeat. "I'm sorry, but I don't want to be your husband."

"What's going on?" Her gaze bounced from Jason to Mimi, who was off to the side of the set, eyes bugging out like somebody had just given her a pony or a diamond-encrusted filing cabinet.

Jason stepped toward Hazel and lowered his voice. The sound engineers positioned around the edges of the stage scrambled to lower their microphones closer to the couple.

"I've made a lot of mistakes," Jason said. "But I don't want to pile them on top of each other. Our marriage would be built on a foundation of lies and ratings, and… I can't do it. I just don't feel that way about you."

Hazel's cheeks were red, and her spine straightened. "After all I have done to get here? You're going to do this to me now?"

Hazel wailed, a high-pitched screech that had the crew scrambling to get their microphones up and out of harm's way as the sound echoed throughout the warehouse. As her gaze shot around the room, she reached down and slipped off her sandal. She positioned it in her hand so the hard wedge was pointing out and rushed toward Jason in a show of unbridled fury.

She landed on top of him with a barbaric scream, hitting him with the shoe until he covered his face with his hands and curled into a ball on the stage.

"I'll make you pay!" she screamed. "I know people."

I followed her gaze to the back of the room, craning my neck just in time to see a shock of red hair disappear around the corner.

After watching the scene unfold with undisguised glee,

Mimi flipped a switch on her headset and serenely said, "Security, please."

Two men dressed in all black approached the stage, followed closely by Hollis and Gage, who had just entered from the back.

"Miss Archer," Hollis said, his arms locking around her waist. Her hair had come loose from its updo and was sticking out sideways in a tempestuous sprayed clump. Her eyes flashed wildly, and she was struggling against him. "You need to come with us."

Hazel reared back and glared at Hollis. "What do you mean? I haven't done anything."

Hollis eyed the camera and shook his head slowly. "I'm afraid we need to ask you some questions."

"You're questioning me?" she screamed. "For what? Fighting with my boyfriend? He tried to dump me on the day of our—"

She squirmed free from Hollis and rushed across the stage again.

He took two large steps and intercepted her again. He pulled a pair of handcuffs from his belt and wrapped one side around her wrist. When he twisted her arms behind her and fastened the other cuff, a harsh metallic snap reverberating through the set. "For hiring Jeff Kapowski to falsify and post libelous information about Lily Page on his blog."

Lily stumbled backward, her eyes wide. "That was you?"

"Of course not." Hazel's self-indulgent smile turned brittle as Hollis prodded her out the door. "I wouldn't waste my money on you."

~

AFTER HOLLIS ESCORTED Hazel off the stage, Jason took a seat in the front row. Within minutes, two of Hazel's friends jumped up to comfort him, and he offered the camera a lopsided grin.

Mimi stepped forward and tapped the director on the shoulder. "May I speak with you privately?"

He dutifully followed her to the back of the set, and even though they were partially hidden by a row of potted silk palms, we all openly stared as he shook his head and she emphatically tapped her clipboard.

When she advanced a few moments later, Mimi was rubbing her palms together, her eyes bright. "As they say in Hollywood, the show must go on. Javier, if you could have everyone take their places."

They started filming where they left off, minus one-half of the competitors. Javier made a dramatic presentation of pulling the slip of paper out and waving it around with a flourish. "The winners of *Romance Revival*, including a five hundred-thousand-dollar cash prize and the wedding of a lifetime, are Dan and Lily."

Half the crowd applauded. The other half complained the vote was rigged and demanded to see proof that Lily and Dan had actually won instead of getting the prize because Hazel was disqualified for being a petulant attention hog.

The camera panned the room, capturing chaos in every corner. Grandmothers yelled at the photographers, cousins knocked over light stands, and an unsuspecting caterer tried to convince Hazel's sorority sisters it was too early for the booze he had hidden behind a soundbar.

Through it all, Mimi stood with her fingertips pressed to her lips, failing to conceal a triumphant grin.

After a few moments, Caroline ushered a wide-eyed Lily off the stage, steering her past the mayhem and into the dressing room.

Javier stepped to the microphone and tapped it, sending a resonant thump through the speakers. He gave a brittle laugh. "Now that I have your attention, we'll let the bride and groom get ready, and then we'll begin the ceremony."

I stopped in front of Maggie, who appeared to be guarding a plant at the front of the stage. She lowered her voice to a whisper and peered over my shoulder. "These people are insane. The lady in the feathered corset was about to use an asparagus fern as a weapon."

"We're almost done," I said with a sigh. "Let's just get through the wedding. I've got Lily. You find Dan."

When I turned the corner, Lily was standing with her back against the wall and her eyes closed. Caroline and Beverlee whispered to her in hushed tones.

I cleared my throat. "They promised you a day you'd never forget."

She tucked her arms around her waist, the crown of flowers slipping over her forehead as she nodded. "I knew Hazel was petty and vindictive, but I can't believe she paid someone to post those stories about me."

"It wasn't entirely about you," Beverlee said. "I saw Hollis on his way in, and I might have coerced him into giving me a few details."

She gave a quick shimmy.

"Who was it about, then?" I asked.

"It was about Hazel," she replied. "Hollis has a phone recording of Hazel offering the photographer money to make her a more prominent feature on the tabloid site."

"She hired someone to stalk herself?" Caroline asked. "That's nuts."

"On top of that," Beverlee said, leaning in with a conspiratorial whisper, "she made threats against Lily on the recording. Something about pulling her hair out by the roots and slapping her bald head on a stake *Lord of the Flies*-style before the premiere."

Lily gasped, and her hand flew to her hair. "She said that? About me? But I thought we were becoming friends."

I handed her a lipstick for a quick touch up. "Girls like Hazel are all bluster. I don't think she would actually do it. Would she?"

Before Lily could respond, Mimi appeared at the door and tapped her watch.

"Showtime," I said, then leaned in toward Lily. "Are you sure you want to do this?"

When Dan rounded the corner and reached out his hand, she released a deep breath and took a hesitant step toward him. "I don't know. Am I?"

Dan took her hand in his, then pulled it in to rest on his chest. "Lily, I'm truly sorry for letting you go. I made a choice based on fear, rather than love."

A cameraman scrambled to get in position, leaning in close to the pair.

Lily bowed her head. "But your family…"

"I'd like for *you* to be my family, if you'll have me," he replied. "And if my father doesn't approve, he can kick me out of the business. I might end up poor, but at least I'll be with you."

He engulfed her in a hug, then dropped to the floor at her feet. "Lily Page, will you marry me?"

She eagerly agreed, and Beverlee let out a loud whoop. She dabbed a tissue to her eyes. "I love a happy ending."

Caroline wrapped her arm around her sister's waist. "You see? I told you it would work out for you. It always does."

She straightened the straps of Lily's dress. "Let's go get you married."

"Okay, then." I pointed toward the door. "I believe there's a giant swing with your name on it."

〜

THE SET DESIGNERS had built a catwalk into the overhead system of scaffolding so they could lower Lily to the stage with dramatic flair. To reach the top, she had to climb a rickety metal ladder that conjured up memories of the rusty tools in my great-grandpa's shed.

I examined the ladder, then glanced over at Lily. "Are they serious? It wasn't in the budget to build you steps?"

Lily bent down to pick up the ends of her long dress. "I told them it was fine. I've been climbing trees since I was knee high to a fire ant. But I will need somebody to help me keep from stepping on this on the way up," she said with a grin.

"Don't you have a sister for something like that?" I glanced over at Caroline, who was studying her fingernails.

"Not likely," Caroline said. "I've never been the tree-climbing type. And besides, I need to be on stage to ooh and ahh over your grand entrance with the rest of the guests."

Lily hiked her skirt even higher, then stepped a bare foot on the bottom rung. "Ready?"

"Ready as I'll ever be," I said with a barely concealed eye roll.

She made the ascent slowly, and I followed, her behind and a pillowy mass of gown obstructing my view. I was practically inside her wedding dress, a position many people would have liked to be in, but I couldn't wait to escape.

"Almost there," she said from above me.

When she neared the top, a member of the production crew strapped her into the waist harness hand-sewn into the bodice of her dress and got her settled on the wide wooden swing.

I trailed her, clinging to the rail as I peered twenty feet down at the stage while my breakfast pitched back and forth in my stomach.

"Are we all set up there?" the director called from his position next to the stage.

The crew member gave a nod as he slowly began releasing the swing.

From below, Javier spoke the familiar words of the ceremony. "Friends and family, we are gathered here together to celebrate the marriage of Daniel Foster Nichols to Liliana Grace Page. Please rise for the presentation of the bride."

"That's your cue," I whispered to Lily as guests rose to their feet. "Good luck."

She gave me a shy smile and wrapped her fingers around the ropes on both sides of the swing. Behind the scenes, a muscle-bound man in a black t-shirt and jeans used an intricate pulley system to lower her to the stage.

The Wedding March played through the speakers, and every set of eyes in the room focused on Lily as she descended from the clouds.

Even Dan, who had been shifting back and forth and eying the exit sign earlier, was transfixed. When he saw Lily, he straightened his tie.

"That's right, buddy," I whispered. "Don't mess this up."

Javier approached the center of the stage. "True love isn't easy to find. And it is with great joy that we join together today to celebrate—"

A chair scraped loudly across the floor. "True love?" a loud voice boomed. "What do you know about true love?"

I craned my head to see Odell Page, Lily's father, barreling toward the stage. His long black overcoat flapped behind him, and in his right hand, he was waving around a shotgun.

The swing came to a sudden stop five feet above the ground, the stagehand gripping the rope between his leather-gloved hands. Lily swayed back and forth until Dan circled his hand around her ankle to slow the movement.

"This isn't love." Odell halted in front of Dan. He lifted the gun as if he were waving a flag. "You lie like a dog licking Thanksgiving dinner off my mama's linoleum floor. And I will kindly implore you to take your hands off my daughter."

"Daddy," Lily cried, her fingers white from her tight hold on the ropes. "Stop."

"I will do no such thing, young lady. You need to get down from there right now."

Dan stepped forward, reaching out to the man who was about to become his father-in-law. "Sir, if we could talk about this…"

Odell's face whipped around toward Dan, his eyes flaming. He rested the butt end of the shotgun on the floor but kept his hand on the barrel. "Does this seem like a good time to talk, son?" With each syllable, he raised and lowered the gun with a thunk on the wood.

Guests rushed toward the exits as the security team approached the set.

Mimi held her hand up to stop their progression, then motioned for the cameras to keep rolling.

I slid along the catwalk and started to descend toward the stage.

Lily, still suspended over the scene, screamed to get her father's attention. "Daddy, no! Let me get down, and we'll figure it out."

Odell turned back to Lily. He lifted the arm holding the shotgun into the air. "You can't possibly tell me you want to marry this fool, Princess. I won't allow it."

Lily leaned forward on the swing, meeting her father's eyes. "I want what you and Mama had," she replied with a delicate sniff. "And yes. I want to marry him."

Just then, Mimi gave a quick nod to the security guard, who lunged in and wrapped his arms around Odell. Odell twisted to evade him, his finger grazing the shotgun's trigger.

A deafening crack reverberated through the room. Broken glass rained to the floor at the back of the stage where Odell's bird shot took out yet another chandelier.

Screams filled the air and people dove for cover, including the stagehand holding the loose end of the rope. The wood swing crashed to the ground with a bang.

Lily landed in a heap of white tulle next to her father, her crown of yellow flowers resting crookedly across her forehead.

I rushed to help Lily to her feet as she watched the second person of the day be carted off by the police.

~

WHILE THE CREW cleaned up the broken glass, we converted the wardrobe room into an impromptu bridal suite.

Maggie sat in the makeup chair next to me, her eyes wide. "I have seen a lot of things at weddings. But this one tops them all."

I tried to hold back an adrenaline-fueled laugh. "I almost wet myself when that chandelier fell. I think I'm going to steer clear of elevated light fixtures for a while."

Lily and Caroline huddled together on the sofa. "Do you think he'll go to jail?" Lily asked, her voice trembling.

"He was brandishing a weapon," Beverlee said. "In the middle of a crowd of people."

Maggie shrugged. "I've seen fathers do crazier things during their daughters' weddings. There's so much tension— they're giving their little girls away to other men. It can all be very emotional. I once had a father hire out an exorcist to disrupt the ceremony."

"If you need an exorcist, you've got bigger problems than your daughter getting married." Beverlee rifled through the drawers in the makeup station, whooping in triumph when she found a snack-sized bag of animal crackers. She offered one to Lily. "Mimi wouldn't dare say anything to you about crumbs in your teeth now."

My ribs felt as if they had been hollowed out with a rusty pocketknife, but I couldn't imagine eating. I leaned back and squeezed my eyes closed until stars exploded behind my lids.

"Do you think he's behind the... other issues?" Lily asked, her voice tentative.

"Daddy?" Caroline asked with a snort. "Not likely. He's a big teddy bear, and as mad as he was, he'd do anything in the world for you. Besides, Hazel all but confessed to being in over her head on her way out of here earlier."

"It doesn't sit right with me, though," I said. "How did Hazel know the show wouldn't be canceled after Beau died? And what did she have against Rocco? He made her skin as smooth as porcelain."

I studied the women's somber faces, noting that nobody had any answers. But I had to find some way to rescue the wedding, so I forced my best attempt at enthusiasm. "Enough about that. Today's supposed to be a day of celebration, which begs the question: are you still going through with it?"

Lily blinked in surprise. "Going through with what? The wedding?"

Almost afraid to hear the answer, I gave her a hesitant nod.

"Well, yes, I guess. Mimi came by here earlier and reminded me I signed a contract."

Beverlee laughed. "I would imagine you could get out of that. Your life was in danger. Killing both of their stars wouldn't be good publicity."

Lily smoothed a shaking palm down the front of her dress. "I'm already dressed, and I have a groom," she replied, reaching down to squeeze her sister's hand. "I want to get married today."

We sat in awkward silence, wondering how much punishment one woman was willing to endure for a trip down the aisle, until Beverlee jumped up and hooted. "This calls for a toast to the beautiful and resilient bride."

I scanned the room, but the only thing available for a toast was a can of diet soda that had been sitting open on the makeup counter since before Rocco died.

"I think I saw some champagne on the props table," Caroline suggested.

Beverlee clapped. "Wonderful. Why don't you and Glory grab it, and I'll get Lily freshened up for the ceremony?" She started pawing through the drawers.

Caroline hopped up and headed toward the exit, but I stopped with my hand on the doorframe. "You know, Lily, I don't think you give yourself enough credit. You're kind and generous, and you and Dan deserve every happiness."

"Reminds me of someone else I know," Beverlee said with a wink.

She topped off Lily's mascara, ran a fluffy powder brush over her cheeks, and straightened the floral crown. "You really are a stunning bride," Beverlee said. "And I've had a lot of weddings. I should know."

Just then, Mimi brushed past me through the door. She tapped her finger on her clipboard. "Grab the champagne, then. We've got to get back to filming. Union rules say we need to have the camera guys out of here in an hour or we owe them overtime."

Lily took a deep breath and stood from the sofa. "I'm ready." She straightened her shoulders and followed Mimi out the door.

22

The props room was on the opposite side of the warehouse from the ceremony set, and it housed everything from plush sofas to high-dollar fashion accessories. If it could transform an empty cinder block cell into a restaurant or make a stretch of sand appear to be an exclusive island paradise, *Romance Revival* designers stashed it there.

I stepped around a six-foot-tall inflatable beer bottle poking out from the seat of an antique oak church pew and found Caroline filling red plastic cups with expensive champagne.

"We should be using fancy glass flutes," she said, tapping the plastic with her finger. "But these were all I could find on short notice."

I grinned and reached for a cup from the tray. "Looks good to me. Doesn't matter what the bubbles come in as long as they make their way into my belly."

When I raised it toward my lips, Caroline jerked the cup away from me, sloshing a couple dollars' worth of champagne on the tile floor at my feet.

"No," she said sharply. "You can't drink it yet."

"Why? They won't mind if we steal a sip before the ceremony," I said. "And besides, this might be our only chance to toast this crazy day. Mimi's ready to get started."

Caroline grabbed a thick stack of paper towels from the wall dispenser and dropped them on the ground in front of us. She squatted and mopped up the spilled liquid with short, violent strokes. "I said you can't drink it. It's bad luck."

I didn't think drinking champagne before a ceremony was bad luck. Usually, it made the day flow more smoothly. A slightly boozy bride didn't fret over the details. But I held out my palm, surrendering. Whatever was bugging Caroline wouldn't be fixed by an argument. "It's not a problem. We'll save it for later."

She scrubbed the floor until she left a noticeably clean spot in the linoleum, then tucked the used paper towels in her backpack and marched toward the sink to scrub her hands.

I turned to the exit, but as my gaze swept over the drink tray, something caught my eye. The plastic cup I'd relinquished sat away from the others. On its side, almost so small I couldn't see it, a small black dot had been drawn on the plastic.

An uncontrollable shiver rippled through me. It wasn't that Caroline didn't want me to drink a cup of champagne. She just didn't want me to drink that particular cup of champagne.

I remembered the night of the party when Caroline had collapsed. The videos hadn't shown an ill-intentioned stranger near the drinks because there hadn't really been anyone else around.

Only Caroline had free access to her glass.

Caroline. The same woman who noted that she was less than two hours away from Flat Falls the day of the murder on an evening when nobody would have noticed her late return.

The woman who always trailed behind her beautiful younger sister, watching as Lily soaked in her father's attention and caused a media frenzy.

I sucked in a ragged breath. Caroline hadn't been the victim of a crime—she had put the drugs in her own drink.

I pivoted around slowly. "It was you."

With a burst of nervous laughter, she fumbled under her skirt and unsheathed a knife from a holster strapped to her thigh. "Daddy was right. A lady should never go out unprepared. You never know when you'll need to cut someone."

She motioned to the other side of the room with a sharp nod.

I tried to rush past her, but her hand shot out, the knife slicing deeply through my upper arm. A hot flash of pain dropped me to my knees. Blood splashed across the floor, and I sucked in a low hiss as the walls began to pirouette in my peripheral vision.

I glanced up when a low creak sounded in the doorway, and Jeff stepped in, his hoodie now replaced with a crisp button-up and a thin blue tie.

"Oh, thank goodness." I tried to clear my head with a quick shake, but it left me breathless, and the walls were still spinning. "You've got to help me."

A soft chuckle escaped his lips as he closed the door behind him. "What seems to be the problem?" he asked, the lock engaging with a deafening snap.

Caroline crossed the room to his side, and he wound his hands through her hair, reeling her in for a kiss.

"Wait," I said, the rasp of my voice unfamiliar. "You two know each other?"

Caroline smiled. "We were high school sweethearts."

"But—"

"We even went to the prom together." She dipped her lashes and offered him a demure giggle.

I pointed toward Jeff, forcing myself not to look at my dripping arm. "This is the dorky prom date? The glitter truck guy?" I asked with an ill-timed chuckle.

Caroline charged forward, her palm cracking against my cheek. "Don't you dare speak about him that way."

I opened my mouth to respond, but terror kept the words from coming out.

"Jeff knows what it feels like to be the butt of everyone's jokes," she went on. "But who's laughing now?"

I whipped my head toward Jeff. "You were humiliated in high school, so you run a gossip website now to return the favor?"

"It's one of the perks of the job," he admitted, a slow smile crossing his face.

"You did all this to humiliate Lily in retribution for embarrassing you in high school?"

He choked out a derisive chuckle as he zipped his camera bag closed, then he lifted his hands up. "That was all Caroline. I'm just along for moral support. And to upload the stories she feeds me."

"Why?" I asked Caroline, blinking several times to regain my focus.

"You don't have a sister, do you?"

I shook my head, glancing around the room for a makeshift weapon. Most of the heavy props, like the thick iron candelabras Maggie and I had argued over including on the cake table, had been moved to the set. Only bolts of fabric and random pieces of farmhouse decor remained. I couldn't figure out how to save myself with a two-foot section of shiplap, no matter how hard I tried.

"I didn't plan to kill Beau, honestly," she said, staring at the blade in her hand. "I just wanted to rough him up so he wouldn't go through with the wedding. I wanted him to walk out on Lily so she'd be embarrassed on national television."

Understanding washed over me. "To humiliate her the way she humiliated Jeff."

She ran her finger over the edge of the blade slowly, like she savored the pinprick of blood that appeared on her skin. "I didn't even saw all the way through the rope."

"How did you even get in there that day?" I asked. "There was security all over the place."

Jeff lifted the camera from a strap around his neck. "Those dollar store guards were easily distracted."

I swung my head toward Caroline. "And you just... broke in?"

She tore her gaze away from Jeff and leveled me with an annoyed stare. "It wasn't hard. There are open vents all over the back side of the building."

Since I had snuck in here dozens of times myself over the years, I knew that piece of information firsthand.

"And nobody saw you on the set?"

She shook her head. "The crew was on a lunch break."

I jabbed my pointer finger in the air, woozy at the red stain on my sleeve. "So you cut through the rope holding up the chandelier just to scare him?"

"Not all the way through," she reminded me, scraping the tip of the knife under her fingernail before lifting a shoulder. "The cast returned sooner than I expected. I'm surprised it came down that fast, though. I guess I underestimated how much chandeliers weigh."

"And then Rocco, the one with the pretentious hair and swoony eyes, went sniffing around my sister," she continued. "After I got out of the hospital, I went to see him. He told me he had figured out who killed Beau."

I jerked my head up. "He knew it was you?"

"No, he thought it was Jeff and wanted to ask me to help

him keep Lily safe from the 'evil photographer' until he could get enough evidence to take to the police. So I dropped some roofies in his water bottle. When I left, he was stripping his clothes off and dancing with a lamp. Guess that party didn't last long."

With a snort, she leaned against the wall. "Took my entire stash of pills, actually. Lily's Italian Stallion had quite a tolerance. I had to ask Jeff to call in a favor so I could pick up a few more at the last minute. Paid a pretty penny for them —the market for GHB is hot in these parts."

"Why did you drug yourself, then?" I asked, trying to make sense of it all. "You could have died."

"But I didn't," she admonished. "Because I'm not stupid. We calculated the dose carefully. I ingested just enough to get the attention on me for once, but not enough to do any permanent damage. Thank you, science class."

I got a C in science, but I must have been absent the day they taught the crazy girls how to use poison.

Caroline pointed the tip of her knife at a heavy metal bench mounted on the floor at the far side of the room. "Sit."

I pushed myself to my feet and stumbled toward it on wobbly legs.

Caroline pulled a section of thick gaffers tape from a cabinet drawer and wound it tightly around my wrists, binding my hands and ankles to the bench's sturdy supports.

My fingertips tingled, and within seconds, numbness crept up my arms. "I don't have a sister, but I wouldn't try to kill her if I did."

"Oh, I'm not going to kill her," she replied, turning toward me with an ice-cold stare. "You are."

She nodded to the tray of plastic cups. "Sweetie, will you grab those for me? Glory asked me to deliver them to the bride before she took off." She tsked under her breath. "Poor thing, she seemed upset. Said something about her plans not working out the way she wanted."

"You can't do that," I screeched. "Nobody will believe—"

She plucked the drugged cup of champagne off the tray, grabbed my chin between her ice-cold fingers, and emptied the entire thing into my mouth.

"This will all be over soon," she said, pressing a section of tape to my mouth. "And don't worry—you'll be passed out when we dump your body in the water. You won't feel a thing."

She linked her arm through Jeff's. "Sorry to leave you like this, but we have a celebration to attend."

~

After Caroline scurried out of the room, I nearly dislocated my shoulder trying to peel the edge of the tape from my mouth.

When I finally got the corner free, champagne gushed down my face and across my shirt.

I screamed until my throat burned, but nobody heard me. The entire staff was down at the other end of the warehouse, watching the ceremony.

Shifting my body weight back and forth, I tried to tip the bench over, but it didn't budge.

A whacked-out murderer was about to kill one of my brides on national television, and I had no way to stop her.

I was stuck.

I could imagine the scathing testimonial. If I lived through the day, nobody would ever hire me again.

My head sagged toward my chest, and I had almost succumbed to the swirling darkness gathering in my skull when I saw movement just inside the door.

Beverlee's colorful tote bag shimmied forward and backward on the floor, a stream of garbled cackles escaping every time it smacked against the block wall.

Matilda.

A burst of energy surged through me, thankful that Beverlee had picked this room to store her chicken in during the ceremony.

I squealed to get Matilda's attention. No luck. I tried tapping my toes, but because my ankles were fastened to the chair legs, I didn't make much of a racket.

Frustrated, I whipped my head from side to side. Was I seriously trying to convince a chicken to help me escape from a killer? It wasn't like she could hop up on my lap with a tiny switchblade and cut the tape.

With an embarrassed groan, I remembered the noise Beverlee made when she was teaching Matilda to perform tricks. I clucked my tongue against the roof of my mouth. The movement in the bag stilled, but Matilda didn't appear.

I thrust my chin out, exposed my neck, and forced the loudest click I could summon from the back of my throat.

An excited, high-pitched squawk reverberated inside the bag until Matilda's black feathered head popped out through the unzipped end. She wiggled free and jumped out of Beverlee's purse, feathers flying.

I blinked and clicked again.

Matilda ran through the room, releasing an eager buck-buck-buck noise. She hopped on top of a rolled-up velvet Elvis painting before strutting her way across the floor to a ceramic planter shaped like a human nose. She bounced around, pecking the flesh-colored nostril for two solid minutes.

I motioned with my head for her to come closer, oddly disappointed when she didn't even squint in my direction.

Since Matilda didn't speak body language, I clicked louder.

The volume of Matilda's clucks and cackles increased, but she still didn't acknowledge me.

While Matilda ran around in a frenzy, leaving little footprints in the puddle of blood on the floor, I wagged my head and kept clucking.

Just when I was about to give up or pass out from all the chicken chatter, the door flung open.

Josie stood there, eyes frantically searching the room. When her gaze landed on me, she rushed in. "I should have known you'd be in the middle of all this ruckus. It sounded like somebody was having a farm animal pageant in here."

She ripped the rest of the tape off my mouth in one quick motion, and I fought not to scream. "Josie, what are you doing here?"

"I figured it out," she said, rubbing her hands up and down my arms to restore the circulation. "I know who killed my husband. It was—"

"Lily's sister," I finished.

Josie nodded and peeled a lingering strip of tape from my wrist. "I spent the morning following the trail from those printouts Rocco had."

I gaped at her. Most of us spent our free time knitting or eating entire bags of peanut M&M's. Josie hacked into other people's computers.

"What?" She shrugged. "I was bored. But during my digging, I discovered that the guy who runs the *Enchanted Tattler* is from Lily's hometown."

"He had a personal vendetta against her," I said, bending my fingers to make sure they all still worked. "High school humiliation leaves a deep scar."

Josie dropped the ball of tape from my wrist onto the ground, and Matilda immediately got it stuck to the outside of her beak.

"But I found something else when I was poking around

on the server. I discovered a series of emails leaking information about Lily's affair to the tabloids."

"Caroline," I replied with a nod.

"That's how Jeff and Caroline reconnected. She was looking to unload the video of Lily and her dirty fling, and he was her inroad to Tabloidville." She pursed her lips. "Speaking of which, that man really needs to update his firewall. That thing had more holes than my ex-husband's underwear."

"But why would she do it? Money?"

Josie shook her head and pressed a folded paper towel onto my arm. "She didn't ask for money; she only wanted to ruin her sister."

I jerked my chin up with a hiss, grabbing the bench to steady my wobbly vision. "But what other reason could there be for Caroline to do that to her sister?"

"Jealousy?" Josie suggested, lifting the towel to peek underneath. "Lily was a small-town princess. Men loved her, and she was Daddy's favorite. If I had a real-life Cinderella for a sister, I'd probably hate her, too. Maybe Caroline wanted some attention all to herself for a change."

"And she's about to get it. She was on her way to the ceremony." I jumped up and staggered toward the door, fighting the wooziness that threatened to bring me crashing to the ground. Just before I stepped into the hallway, I turned back. "I thought you couldn't leave the house," I said, gesturing to her leg. "How did you—"

She hiked up her long floral skirt to display a ring of raw, red skin around her ankle. "YouTube—you wouldn't believe the things you can learn to do with plastic bags and quality hand lotion."

I jerked the tape from Matilda's beak and scooped her up. Once I got her safely zipped inside Beverlee's tote, I thrust the bag out to Josie. "Come on," I said. "You take the chicken. I have to save my bride."

∽

WE RACED down the hallway as Javier's voice boomed over the loudspeaker. "I now pronounce you husband and wife. You may kiss the bride."

Cheers erupted through the crowd.

As we wove past cameras and people, nearly falling into the cake table set up along the back wall, Caroline stepped toward the microphone. "Let's have a toast. Does anyone need a refill? The wedding planner left us an extra bottle." She held up the champagne. "It's not the good stuff, but it will have to do."

I grunted. That champagne cost more than my car.

"Here's to forever," Caroline said, a smile creeping across her face.

"Cheers," Lily replied, lifting the glass to her mouth.

"No!" I screamed and raced down the aisle toward the couple, launching myself at Lily and knocking the cup out of her hand. It splashed to the wood floor, soaking the silk runner Maggie had laid down with such precision under Mimi's watchful glower.

Maggie glared at me from the other side of the room. "Sorry," I said, stumbling to my feet. "But you can't drink that."

"Why not?" Caroline lifted her own cup and took a healthy swig, turning to me with a satisfied smirk. "There's nothing wrong with it. And every bride needs champagne on her wedding day."

I stepped across the stage toward Lily, who was watching me with a combination of fear and surprise. "I don't want to be the one who ruins your ceremony," I whispered, my

237

stomach rocking as I surveyed the piles of broken furniture and debris littering the set. "Although surely I'm not at the top of that list today."

Josie cleared her throat from the front row.

"Right," I said, shaking the cobwebs from my head. I pointed toward Caroline. "It was your sister. She killed Beau and Rocco."

"Me?" Caroline gasped and placed a hand across her stomach. "That doesn't even make sense. Don't forget, somebody tried to kill me, too."

I hesitated, my chest tightening. I'd always wanted a sister, and ruining their relationship was more difficult than I had imagined. "She's jealous of you, Lily. You have everything she wants. Love. Happiness. Your father's attention. She slipped the drug in her own drink that night so everybody would focus on her for a change."

Caroline's eyes darted toward the exit. "It's not true, Lily. Who are you going to believe, your only sister or the woman who can't even pull together a real wedding cake?"

Bewildered, Lily lifted the hem of her dress and took two steps backward. "I don't…"

Dan put his arm around his new wife's back, pulling her close to his chest.

When Jimbo strode out on the stage, his security badge firmly in hand, Caroline leaped off the front of the platform, stumbling to a stop in the middle of the aisle. "You had it coming to you," she said.

Lily gasped. Her voice shook, and tears spilled down her washed-out cheeks. "But… why? What did I ever do to you?"

"Everything," she replied, backing toward the exit with measured steps. "You were the beautiful one. The smart one. Mama's favorite. And the only one Daddy paid attention to."

I ventured in front of her with outstretched hands. "Caroline, put the knife down."

"No," she sneered, the metal glinting under the bright studio lights as she waved it in the air. "I'm done with you, Lily. When Mama died, it broke Daddy's heart, and he decided he had to fix you. So anything pretty Lily wanted, pretty Lily got. All I got was the leftovers. Isn't that right?"

Lily gave a mirthless chuckle. "No. You seem to forget it hasn't been all sunshine and roses for me either."

Caroline threw her head back and made an odd squealing sound. When her chin bobbled up and down, I realized it was laughter. She gestured toward Dan. "Are you talking about getting busted playing with the devil's toadstool at the pickle factory? Who do you think sent those pictures to the tabloids, sister dearest?"

Lily recoiled like Caroline had slapped her. "That was you?"

"It's about time you learned you can't have everything you want."

Just then, Dan groaned and slumped to the floor, his empty cup of champagne clattering to the floor.

"What have you done?" Lily screamed, falling to the ground next to Dan.

"Call 911," I yelled. As the flustered crowd rushed around, I turned to Josie. "You need to go. If you get caught here, you'll be in even more trouble."

She nodded, then sprinted to the back exit.

I glanced up to find Caroline taking slow steps toward Lily, the knife in her hand still sticky with my blood. "Look out!" I cried.

Just before Caroline got within arm's reach of her sister, I saw a streak of pink out of the corner of my eye. I turned to see Beverlee, arms outstretched, launching the top tier of the Styrofoam wedding cake at Caroline's back.

Icing roses flew around the room like miniature torpe-does, landing in colorful mounds on the first few rows of guests. Mimi used her clipboard to deflect one when she saw it hurtling toward her face.

Caroline fell to the ground with a thud, and the knife clattered to the floor next to her. I kicked it away with my foot.

Beverlee flashed a toothy grin. "I was afraid she was going to stab the bride. And you can't get blood out of a wedding gown. Trust me, I know."

Jimbo stepped between them with a plastic bag of cable ties. As he was removing one, he screeched and jumped on a bench in the front row, pointing down the aisle at Matilda, who had escaped from the handbag and was pecking at a pile of fondant that was stuck on Caroline's shoe.

Beverlee clicked her tongue once, and Matilda hopped onto her thigh, turning to face me with a high-pitched squawk.

I scowled at the chicken. "Why couldn't you do that earlier?"

The day's events had not left a surface untouched. Glass fish bowls sat in broken piles under dangling strings of long-extinguished twinkle lights. Fabric curtains sagged in tattered shreds. Cracks lined the fake windows, and the ice sculpture Eiffel Tower rested on its side, a trail of melted water seeping out of it like blood. I broke off the top platform and held it against my cut.

Hollis stepped in from the back of the set and cocked his head to the side as he examined the carnage, letting out a knowing grunt when his gaze locked with mine. He pulled out a pad of paper and started questioning the guests, while Lily rested her forehead against Dan's chest and watched in silence as Gage carted her sister off to the police station.

"I don't have enough room in my jail for all of your colleagues, Glory," Hollis said, scrubbing his fingers across his scalp.

I lifted a shoulder. I couldn't have predicted this kind of ending. I had never seen a wedding filled with that much chaos end with the bride and groom holding hands. Not even on TV.

As I turned to start the clean-up process, I passed by Mimi, who stood next to the podium with her clipboard, a smear of frosting across its center. "That was wild," she said to the cameraman at her side. "I hope you caught every ridiculous minute of it."

23

Two weeks later, I sat on the sofa in Josie's living room, squished between Beverlee and Scoots. Snacks filled the coffee table in front of us and spilled over onto trays on the floor.

In true Beverlee fashion, she had spent the day cooking, and because she wasn't sure if we were celebrating or weeping, she'd brought enough food for both.

From thick slabs of homemade sourdough smeared with fresh goat cheese and sprigs of dill to gooey caramel brownies, no food group had gone ignored in her quest to meet my every emotional need.

I turned to Josie, who sat with her feet tucked under her on a chair beside us. "How did it go with your correctional officer?" I asked, then pointed to the monitor she had slid back onto her ankle, courtesy of a jar of petroleum jelly and an impressive number of Popsicle sticks for leverage. "Did they ever bust you for leaving the house?"

She shook her head and grinned. "No, and he even apologized to me for the confusion around my visit to the health food store. Said he might try becoming a vegan because those tofu burgers sounded so good."

"Does that mean you're not a criminal anymore?" Beverlee asked, popping a cherry tomato stuffed with blue cheese and toasted pecans into her mouth.

"No, I'm still a criminal," Josie replied. "But they've expunged everything related to Beau's death from my record. So I just have to hang out here with you three for the next few months until Lady Justice sets me free."

"Speaking of criminals," Scoots said. "Did Mimi ever confess why she hid the footage from the bachelorette party?"

Mimi had "found" the footage on the afternoon of the final taping, after Hollis threatened her with charges for obstructing his investigation. "She thought a *Romance Revival* crew member committed the murders, and she was worried the police would shut everything down before the finale if they knew."

"That's probably true, but then we wouldn't have had a wedding," Beverlee said. "Speaking of which, have you talked to Lily?" Beverlee asked.

I nodded. "Briefly, when she called to thank me for helping her get through her wedding day. Her father's still not acknowledging her, even though she sweet-talked the judge into dropping the charges against him. She and Dan leave next week for their honeymoon. They're going to start their own pickle empire with the prize money. They seemed... happy."

"Is that a good thing?" Beverlee asked.

"It's good. Given everything that's happened the last few weeks, I think we're all due a little joy."

When a knock sounded at the door, Scoots bent forward and raised a brow. "That must be the joy fairy."

Josie laughed, and with her hair loose around her shoulders and the frown lines gone from her forehead, she seemed peaceful for the first time in ages. "No, just Gage. I invited him over to watch the show."

Beverlee rose and brushed the crumbs off the front of her lime green romper. "That's darn close to a joy fairy. But we didn't realize we were interrupting. We can go."

Josie nudged Beverlee back toward the sofa with her shoulder before crossing to the door. "No need. You guys are family."

Gage didn't seem surprised to see us, but his eyes widened at the volume of food Beverlee had prepared. He pressed a soft kiss to Josie's cheek and nodded back out at the porch, where Ian stood with his hands in his pockets. "Ian was on his way to see Glory, but when we heard the cackling and smelled the meatballs, we thought you might all be over here."

"Cackling?" Scoots said, raising a breadstick in the air like an extension of her finger. "I'll show you cackling."

Ian stepped through the door, immediately followed by Rusty, who was panting and wagging his tail. "Mind if we join you?"

Beverlee scooted over and patted the small spot next to her on the sofa. "Make yourself comfortable."

Ian cleared his throat. "Thanks, Beverlee, but I don't think I—"

"I wasn't talking to you," she replied with a smirk. "I was talking to the dog."

I rolled my eyes and went to the refrigerator for a bottle of water. I twisted the cap and held it out to him. He took a long sip, then flashed me a lopsided smile. My gaze immediately went to his dimple, and an odd swirl formed deep in my belly.

"Are you ready for your television debut?" he asked.

"Ready as I'll ever be," I said, nervousness bouncing

ERIN SCOGGINS

around my stomach. "They say any publicity is good publicity, right? How bad could it be?"

Beverlee clapped several times from the living room. "Everybody shush, it's starting."

When I rejoined them, Scoots grabbed a bottle of champagne from an ice bucket on the floor, thumbing the cork off with a pop. My chest expanded as I took in my people, all gathered around the television to watch the last episode of the show that would launch my new career as a wedding planner.

I squeezed onto the sofa between Beverlee and Rusty. "Should we have invited Maggie?"

Beverlee wrinkled her nose. "Did you two form a truce while you were working on the show?"

"Maybe." I shrugged. "A little. Turns out she's good at her job."

When the opening credits started to play, Javier McMasters appeared on screen. A red plaid shirt with gold buttons had replaced the purple tuxedo jacket, and he looked like a glammed-up Christmas present.

"What we are about to show you may frighten small children," he said, his voice low and controlled. "If there are little ones around, please put them to bed or lock them in the bathroom. And then join us for the most explosive event in reality television history."

What followed was a preview montage of glass breaking, shotgun blasts, and me, launching myself into the bride's back with blood smeared across my face.

It went downhill from there.

Scoots thrust the bottle of champagne toward me. "Huh. That won't be good for business."

While the footage made me appear to be a highly unstable psychopath with a penchant for ruining weddings,

246

shots of Maggie showed her smiling in a pristine pastel pantsuit, organized portfolio in hand.

The final credits rolled and simply read: Wedding Planning Services by Magnolia Winters and Gloria Weller.

"That's not even my name!" I took a swig from the bottle and pointed it at Beverlee. "No truce. I practically die for this wedding and she gets all the credit?"

Ian grasped my shoulder and gave it a gentle squeeze. "You'll get 'em next time, Glory," he whispered into my ear.

"Next time? I was drugged and almost skewered." I held out my arm for everybody to see the bandage that still covered the battle wound from my stitches. "This wedding scarred me for life. What could possibly happen after this? A bride who wants to get married in the middle of a scorpion tank?"

"That could be fun. Did you know scorpions die from constipation if you pull their tails off? You could be in charge of a stopped-up scorpion wedding." Beverlee grinned and extended a white ceramic tray piled high with smoked salmon and cream cheese stuffed into flaky pastry dough. "Fish puff?"

As I sunk onto the sofa, surrounded by my chosen family and a mouthwatering buffet of pity food, I couldn't help but smile. Maggie may have gotten the accolades this time, but she was likely spending the evening alone with a frozen dinner and her own poor attitude instead of with people that loved her.

Even better, since Mimi couldn't get my name right, Carolina Weddings still had an impeccable reputation. Maggie could take the heat for the chaos. Although this wedding would traumatize all of us for a long time, we ended up with a happily married couple. And that was better than beating Maggie.

At least for now.

ACKNOWLEDGMENTS

Most authors are also avid readers, and it gives me such joy to know my books are in such loving, enthusiastic hands. Readers are the best people, and I offer my sincere gratitude to every book lover who has given their time to join me in Flat Falls. If you were here, I'd invite you onto my front porch for a glass of sweet tea and a plate of Matilda-approved sugar cookies.

I am so very lucky to have a team of people at my side who use their expert skills to help make my stories the best they can be. Thank you to Mariah Sinclair, Stacy Juba, Beth Hale, and Virginia Carey for being my behind-the-scenes superheroes.

A special thank you to the author community, specifically to Liz Tully and the Secondary Characters. While writing can be a solitary journey, I'm so glad I don't have to take it alone.

I'd like to give a huge shout out to my friends and family for being the best cheering section a girl could ask for. To my mom and dad, thank you for being both my most trusted early readers and my most ardent fans. Karen Brock, thanks for the zillion parking lot pep talks and for your continued friendship. Thank you to Diane, Kathy, and the countless others who have encouraged and supported me in ways I couldn't have even imagined.

Finally, to Sean, Miller, Gibson, and Serena, there aren't words for how grateful I am that you are my people. You have clapped the loudest, whooped the most often, and accompanied me down this path with unwavering faith. You have both my thanks and my heart. Always.

ABOUT THE AUTHOR

Erin Scoggins is a long-time Southerner with a fondness for offbeat humor and pickled okra. After fifteen years in marketing with a Fortune 500 company, she traded her MBA for fictional crime scenes and small-town scandals. She writes fun, flirty mysteries that are celebrations of food, family, and the killer South.

Craving something tasty? Nothing beats Beverlee's famous Bless Your Heart Cake.

Visit Erin at www.ErinScoggins.com/cookbook to get your free copy of *'Til Death Do Us Dine*, a collection of Southern snacks, sips, sweets, and stories to help you slay your next celebration.